THE FAMILY

BROKEN WORLD BOOK II

DOUGLAS OWEN

WICKED TALES

THE FAMILY
BROKEN WORLD BOOK TWO
DOUGLAS OWEN

WICKED TALES

HTTPS://WICKEDTALES.CA
A division of DAOwen Publications

The Family / Douglas Owen
Edited by M. J. Moores

ISBN 978-1-928094-49-4
EISBN 978-1-928094-49-7

Jacket Art commissioned by MMT Productions

10 9 8 7 6 5 4 3 2 1

To my family, who have supported me in my writing

PROLOGUE

I have to get Mindy back.

We met the day the world went to shit. And it still amazes me how fast everything came to a halt. The outbreak started in Toronto one day and spread through our world infecting millions in Canada. Being close to the boarder in southern Ontario gave us a little insight on what happened in the United States, but not much. Communication ceased. TV signals went off the air. The electrical grid died. Only those of us prepared with alternate means to power our homes had any form or civilization, and that became short-lived as the dead walked the Earth.

Mindy and I fell in love. But life became a job of survival as we rescued a middle-aged woman named Jill, and she became close with Carl, a truck driving fiend I'm happy to call my friend. I hope he's still alive. But last I saw him, the head of the biker gang that took over Uxbridge put a bullet in his back. I only just escaped. They found us through one of the kids I rescued. Teaches me not to look out for others, but that lesson will never make it through my mind.

A group of us formed a mutual defence against the gang, but Colette was the only one I could save, and together we rescued five-year-old Zoey from being taken for who knows what. The biker gang is organized, more a family than anything else. That's what they call themselves, the family. Pa is the head, really a psychopath looking at controlling as much as he can in this broken world. And he has Mindy, who is carrying my unborn child.

I have to get her back. And somehow we need to survive.

With nowhere to go, I led Colette through the forest of my child-hood and onto the campground my mother ran. Didn't think she survived, but she did. And to make things a little more complicated, a group is with her. I don't know what they're about but all of them survive hunting small game in the forests around the area.

The main drive into the camp is blocked off, and the forest surrounding it laden with home-made land mines and improvised traps. How we managed to get through them without setting any off is unknown to me; I walked in a daze until we came out of the brush near the lake, pushing us hard.

Will we survive? I don't know. Can I save Mindy? Only time will tell, but inside I'm screaming. At least my mother is a bad ass ex-CSIS operative who gave up working for the government to have me and settle down with my father. When he passed away, our relationship became strained. Dad taught me a lot about survival, and Mom made my life a game of figuring things out. She wants to see her grandchild born.

Now we need to make that happen.

HELLO MOTHER

Mother stares down at me with her wrinkled face and crows feet at the corner of her eyes. The curly white hair is new to me, much different than the auburn she kept through my childhood. Her words about me not being able to hold my liquor echoes through my mind.

My eyes ache from the rising sun leaking into her living room from the open door. The crisp spring air helps chase some of the hangover away.

I nod in response to her statement. She always states the obvious, and I could never handle rot gut scotch. The bottle lays on the floor by the couch, not one drop left. Colette should be somewhere, and Zoey as well. Where are they and why was Mom out all night? Those questions need answering.

But after five years of not seeing the woman who gave birth to me, all that came out of my mouth was, "Sure."

Small feet hammer against the stairs followed by heavier ones. Zoey's giant voice slices through the silence as she giggles while running down the steps all wet and covered in suds. Colette follows her, half-soaked and carrying a towel. They both stop before the landing, their gazes dancing between Mom and me.

Zoey lets out a soft whimper and grabs for Colette. The woman reaches down and swoops up the small child, covering her with the blanket.

Mom swings around, pulling out a pistol with one swift movement and kneels. The gun is level and pointing at the two women who came through the forest with me. She pulls back the charging slide, chambering a round, making the weapon hot.

"No!" I automatically put hands to my temples to stifle the pounding.

There's hesitation as Mom puts a hand on her weapon and gently guides the hammer down. The click of the safety thrown on crashes thunder in my ears.

Mom stands and lowers the weapon. "You didn't come in through the road. How did you get in here?"

So like her. No how have you been, what's happened in your life, or concern about me, just how did you get on the property.

"We walked from Island Lake Drive."

Her head turns toward me. "Did you disarm the traps?"

Colette steps off the stairs. "What traps?"

Mom's head snaps back but her shoulders relax after a few seconds. "We have pits and snares, a few landmines, and some trip wires with explosives throughout the woods."

It doesn't register. Not yet. "We walked the same path I used to in order to get to Lazy Lake."

"When you skinny dipped with that girl from Stouffville?" Mom faces me, gun in hand at her side. "Fourteen and always trying to get a girl in bed. Worked out well for you. Word gets around in a small town. That's why you never had a good relationship that lasted any length of time."

"Like you ever did."

It's the old argument again, the one that made me leave home. I stand, my mouth tasting bitter as if someone wiped their butt with my tongue. Drinking always does that to me, especially if I don't brush before going to bed. "Your relationships after Dad lasted what, all of a few days? Don't talk to me about lasting lovers."

Her face turns red, then she is back in control. "I didn't raise you to be a clot. Your dad and me had a great life. Then cancer took him too soon. You know that. Tried to find someone who would accept you, not just me. All the men in the area wanted someone to spread their legs and not have any baggage."

Colette comes down the stairs with Zoey in her arms. Mother's watchful eyes run up and down her. She is calculating, wondering what this woman has to do with me. A few steps and Colette is a little behind me. Zoey grasps at my shoulder but I don't reach back to take her. She stops after a few attempts.

"Your child?" Mom asks.

"Yes, and no."

"Your woman?" Mom nods at Colette.

"No, she's a friend." I turn a little, put a hand behind Colette's back and bring her up beside me. "Colette Robertson, this is my mom, Paulette Patterson. Don't let the soft exterior confuse you, she's about as mean as they come."

Mom snorts. Colette switches Zoey to her left arm and stretches out her right hand.

"Glad to meet you." She winces a little. Mom must have squeezed.

"Well, looks like you have a little one to take care of, so I'll let you have at it. Don't worry about the water, we've a deep well that never goes dry." She looks back at me. "Steve and I'll make some breakfast. It's time to catch up."

———

Mom has a wood burning stove in the kitchen next to a gas one. One burner is black. Split logs are piled to the side and ash decorates the floor under it while the conventional is spotless without even a fingerprint on it, like it got delivered yesterday. She points to the wood one and the fridge against the wall.

"I don't have bacon, but eggs and onions are in the fridge." She opens the stove, grabs a few pages of a yellowed newspaper and starts stuffing it in the thing. "The stove will be ready in a few minutes, just gotta get it up to temp." In go a few logs. "Hand me the matches over there, will ya."

I step to the rear doors at the back of the kitchen, reach out and grab a box of wooden matches. A quick shake and the sound of small pieces of wood rattling tells me its almost full. I take them over to her.

"Thanks," she says without looking up. "Get started on cutting up onions and peppers." A match flairs. "I'll get some eggs from the hen house. Be right back." She stands, watches the fire for a second, nods as the wood catches, closes the stove door, and heads outside.

A knife block sits on the counter. I pull out the utility knife, test the edge, and search for a cutting board. After a few minutes, the onion and peppers I found in the fridge are cut up and ready. One of Mom's cast iron frying pans is heating up on the stove. I find oil in the cupboard and splash a little into it. The cut up vegetables go in as she enters the kitchen, eggs in hand. She puts them on the counter and goes to the fridge, comes back with milk or cream, not sure which. She puts a bit into a bowl and starts cracking eggs into it.

"Simple omelette, just like your dad always made." She whisks the eggs and milk together. "Did you find the sausage?"

I stir the contents of the frying pan. "What are you still doing here?"

"Onions soft yet?" She stops whisking. "I don't like raw onions in my omelette."

"What are you hiding?"

"Nothing." She looks into the pan. "Nope, not ready yet." With that, she returns to the counter, back toward me.

I try again. "How did you survive?"

A couple of eggs crack and the water runs a bit. She's making something else. I don't give up and let the silence continue until she says something.

"When hell started to walk the Earth, I just holed up here with a few people. We kept to ourselves and raided a few places to get going. Got a few cows and hens from a farm on Ninth Line. They're penned up on the east of the pond." She turns with raw dough on a sheet. "From there it was easy. Couple of bikers tried the road in but it's blocked. We have a path that exits out onto Verns Appr Road, the one you made years ago. Covered the exit and dropped some trees with traps in them." She put the sheet in the side of the stove. "Killed a couple of bikers, but made it look like the corpses did it. They don't come back here anymore. The biscuits will take about ten minutes to bake."

"Why the traps north?"

"To keep the others from coming in." She glanced in the pan again. "Almost ready."

Mother is so nonchalant about the apocalypse. Being the only owner of the camp probably made it hard to find out what happened. Even I don't know what went on. But then again, I was not one to pay attention to current events.

"Keep stirring or they'll burn." Mom glances up at me. "Where's your head? I don't like crunchy onions, but I don't like burned ones either." She steps to the counter and returns with a large bowl full of eggs. "Should be enough to make a good-sized omelette. We'll be okay for food this morning."

"We don't have a lot of time." I stir in the eggs, make sure they start to set up, then put the pan on the upper part of the stove. It won't be as hot as the main, so it should cook the eggs evenly.

"And where are you going in such a rush?" Mom checks the biscuits.

"I have to rescue someone from the bikers."

"Who?"

"Mindy." Saying her name makes my voice crack. I don't want to give Mom a lot of information, but she has a way of pulling it out of me.

"And who is she?" Mom stands there staring at me.

Mom is smart. And if I didn't want to involve her, why did I come in search of her? Really, she is older and could have been dead. Was I subconsciously looking for that mother I wanted as a child or the hard-ass bitch who would swat me silly if I did anything foolish?

I tried staring back, but after a while my eyes dried out and the blinking started.

"Let's eat first."

We sit around the table looking at dirty plates. Zoey is only a quick reach away from Colette. I stew on the side between them and Mother, who waits for me to start talking. Before I can say anything, Zoey sits up and stares out the window.

"Who's that?" she asks.

Mom glances outside. "Wilbur, one of the Jackson boys."

"Can I go outside?"

Colette glances at me and I nod. Zoey jumps out of her chair and rushes outside.

"Now we are more comfortable, you can start talking about why you're here and what brought it about." Mom glances at Colette who nods and starts to clear the table.

I take a deep breath and explain my story from the start, that terrible Monday morning drive into work, to meeting Mindy. The death of Frank brings a lump to my throat, but it slides aside at the rescue of Jill. When I come to the point of the first encounter with the bikers Mom is enthralled. Usually, by now she would be asking a dozen questions in machine-gun fashion, but instead she is letting me talk. She smirks a little at the gun club raid, but the smile disappears with the loss of the kid during the adventure.

I describe Pa and what he did to the kids, then the loss of the house, and finally how Mindy was captured. My voice is almost raw. And my hand clutches at the table cloth. I know it's my fault. If I hadn't talked people into watching the fence and making a pain in the ass of myself we could have all moved a little up north or something. The whole biker thing would be in the past. But no, I wanted everyone in their own homes in the community. Hell, we'd have been better off walking to Toronto for all it did.

Mom shakes her head a little and pushes away from the table. I can't read her. She faces the wall, back toward me. Her shoulders rise and fall slightly. She's crying.

I stand, go over to her, and hug. Something I haven't done for years. The surprising thing is she hugs me back. A moment of familial comfort shared between the two of us. My hard-assed Mother has feelings. And not for herself, but her son and a woman she's never met. Something needs to be done, and I now have a warrior on my side. A person trained in just about everything my father could teach her before she had a child. She can shoot, hunt, kill, build, and spit with the best of them. And if she doesn't like something that's in her way, then too bad. She will take it out, just like she did with everything else. No garbage around Paulette Patterson's house, no sir. If you left something out of place it would be thrown out.

We stand there for a while, letting the other be comforted, until she pushes away, wipes at her nose, and goes to the kitchen just as Colette is walking out.

"Dishes are clean," Colette says, brows furrowing at the sight of my now emotional mother. "Is there anything I can do for you?"

"No, just let me alone for a sec." She pushes past the young woman and into the kitchen.

"Did I–"

"No, it wasn't you." I take a deep breath. "Mom may want to help us out with getting our people back."

"That is if there are any people to get back." Her eyes water.

"Your husband." I'm such a jerk. Here I was thinking of only myself while Colette had lost something just as important. We have a commonality of loss that binds our paths.

"We'll get them back," she says. "All of them."

"That we will."

———

I stand beside Mom on the porch as people come strolling in from the cabin area. She has five families living in the camp who help scavenge when they need stuff. We just happened to show up while they were out. Lucky us, for they would have shot on sight.

Mom stands there talking to the group about my arrival with Colette and Zoey. She's a good public speaker and holds the group's attention while explaining the biker threat to the people, making note that they could have been responsible for some of their own losses, especially the young girls. This gets the attention of a few members and they let out a little cry of anger.

Soon, Mom gets to the point of mounting a rescue. "And my son,

Steve, knows where they usually put people to keep them from escaping."

All eyes made me their focus. People waited, looking for information, confirmation, or just hope that their loved ones still survived. Mom nudges me. "Say something."

"Yes, I know where they kept people. I'm sure we could find the other places they keep people by following their pattern." Heads started to nod. "There's a possibility of finding just about everyone who was lost to them." My voice is now firmer. There's a chance. "The biker gang is organized, but their leader lacks vision. All he is out for is to kill anything in his way and to beat up anyone who opposes him."

People nod and glance at one another, as if I'm feeding them something they starve for.

Mom rests a hand on my arm. "Steve can help us a lot. He was trained by the same may who honed my abilities. He knows how to hunt without making noise, can start fires when needed, and has a sound knowledge of firearms."

"Does he know where to get any?" A portly man steps forward. "If we don't have guns then we don't have a chance."

"The Family doesn't have access to the gun clubs yet. Their ammunition must be getting low." Mom steps forward. "After they raided Crappy Tire in Uxbridge I bet they tried the one in Stouffville and Port Perry. We know the one in Stouffville was empty, we did it ourselves. Port Perry is a gamble. Maybe they have some, maybe they don't. I would think others have raided it before the bikers thought of stretching out."

"We have enough for now. Mother showed me what is stored and it should suffice to get us in and out of their holding areas. The best thing we can take in there is a van. A large cargo van with no side windows." I glance around looking for someone who may have an idea of where to find one. Nothing. Not even a slight smile.

"Come on, someone has to know if the dealerships in town has a van like that we could get. Charlie, what about you? You used to work in a dealership." Mom points at a man and stares.

"Yeah, but those types of vans are usually for business. We only had one or two and they'd not even be PDIed yet."

"What would it take to make one of them ready?" I ask.

The man shook his head. "A lift so I could look under it. Maybe change the oil, check the body for problems. Need gas as well. Stuff in the tanks in town is already bad."

"The town has an emergency supply set aside in an air tight storage area," a man points out. "We could use that."

"If it's still there," a woman calls out.

"It's still there, locked up good and tight. All we need is bolt cutters," a middle aged man says.

Mom turns to another man. "Charlie, you have bolt cutters?"

Charlie nods. "Yeah, I got a pair."

"Good, grab 'em and come back here. We need a few people to go on a raid."

Zoey hangs off me like a necklace, a little pendant represented by her legs. It's bad enough telling her I'm heading out for a while, but that she can't go with me is like a needle in her eye. She demands that I let her come. Maybe it's something she's scared of, like losing me, but I can't get her to let go, not when Colette is accompanying me to the raid.

"You need to let go now," I say, trying to pull her arms apart. "I'll be back once we have a van and gas."

She clamps even tighter, threatening to choke me. "I want to go, too."

"If you don't let him go neither of you will be going on the raid," Colette says. "Besides, how am I supposed to hunt for your birthday present if you're with me?"

Zoey lets go of her grip. "How did you know?"

Colette winks. "I know everything, didn't you know that?"

Zoey shakes her head.

"Well, now you do." She gives Zoey a tight hug. "I'll be right back, monkey, and I'll bring the big oaf back with me."

"You promise?" Zoey's large eyes widen.

"Promise."

2

GIFTS

I walk out the door with Colette following. Zoey is pressed up against the window staring after us. It's still spring, and the crisp morning air mists our breath before us. Shadow Lake is covered in a light fog and the grass wets our feet with dew. The sun burnt off the fog from the pond on the other side of the park. All the trees around us hold the fresh, cool morning air as an embrace.

Mom comes barrelling toward us on a noiseless motorcycle. Colette must be thinking the same thing for she's staring at my mother as well, but then again, we've only been here a day. It's a sight, a white-haired older woman riding what looks like a rice burner with no sound emitting from it. She stops just a few feet away.

"Picked these up a few years ago when gas went through the roof. They're great for going into town fast and getting out without attracting the attention of the corpses." She tosses me the keys, a little fob on a ring. "Works using Bluetooth, know what that is?"

I roll my eyes. "Probably better than you do."

"Sure you do. I keep forgetting you're a computer god." She starts to laugh. "Anyway, Jeb and Mark have bikes as well. They're all charged up so you'll have a good four hours of running time." She climbs off the bike. "Standard stuff. Operates just like a gas bike but only two gears, forward and back." She points to the right foot peg with a lever in front. "Down is forward, up is back. Got it?"

"Got it," I say staring at the bike. "This for weapons?" I point to a leather sleeve at the front.

"Yeah." She indicates the one behind the seat. "I put caltrops in this one. Keeps people from following me when I don't want them to."

"Ever drive around Concession three?" I ask, looking to the east.

"Nope, just south into Stouffville and back. Why?"

"Because the bikers have been using them too."

"Makes sense." She reaches into the bag and pulls out a large four-pointed nail. "I started throwing ones like this out just over a year ago, when I was driving the Harley. Damn thing kept attracting corpses faster than you could shake a stick at." She points at the bike. "This one here's a Daymak, best one they built yet. Tricked it out with a spare battery if you run low. Reserve is maybe fifteen to twenty minutes when fully charged."

Colette lifts the seat, her expression still a blank sheet. "Are these the ones?"

"Yes, they are. Just make sure you get back before you use up the charge. The good thing about these bikes is the torque. You can travel through just about anything without worry and still pull yourself out because they're electric. Guess I must have turned green or something."

I nod. "What was your last electric bill, before you cut the grid?"

"Too much." She stops and smiles at me. "Was just over three bills for two months."

"Three hundred? Not bad," Colette says.

"Three thousand," Mom corrects her.

Colette raises an eyebrow. "That's a lot."

"Didn't use any gas here," she says. "Except when I took out Betsy."

"Who's Betsy?" Colette asks.

"The Hog," Mom says. "Really girl, you have to keep your head in the game."

I don't like the way this is going. Mom can lead people into a dark area where she pounces on them to break down their barriers. That's why she was CSIS's best interrogator. Trip up the person to make them reveal their plans and pounce on them. First they want to show they know what they are doing, then they back pedal to prove they're smart, and then she pounces with all the right information, just like a mongoose. You don't expect her to be so crafty, but she is.

"Don't," I say, raising a finger. "We don't need that, not today." I step over and mount the bike. "Come on, Colette, I'll let you in on a few family secretes so you can protect yourself."

We ride down Ninth Line and around Muscleman Lake with jerry cans strapped to the bike. There's a lot of corpses gathered in the lower part of the kettle lake. It's still disturbing to see what used to be people moving around with rot all over them. Skin hangs off bodies and a few birds swoop down and peck at them. Ravens feast on the dead, and most of the corpses crawl in this area. Guess they don't know how to stand. There's a lot of heads sticking out of the water, moving around, trying to make their way toward us. Maybe they followed something into the water or maybe they just honed in on sound. Don't care what it was that got them into the lake, just hope nothing allows them to get out. Wonder if the fish are eating the flesh off the corpses. I used to like fishing. Now, knowing the fish are probably eating the dead, I'll never cast another line in that water again. Probably never will fish again. The thought of eating what feasted on the corpses turns my stomach.

I dodge a couple of car wrecks on the way up the hill. The incline slows us but the corpses following topple over at the steep angle. It's about seven kilometres to Stouffville from Mom's, she's much closer than I was. It brings back the memory of my old home, the one I saved so long for. And with that, Samantha, my cat. Where is she? I miss the little fur ball something fierce. My thoughts wander to Mindy and our unborn child. She's about five months along now, I think. Hard to tell with the days melding into one another. Nothing better have happened to her. Pa's face floats in my mind. He's there, smiling at me as he licks Mindy's cheek. I pull out my Glock, take aim.

"Steve!" Colette yells.

I pull back the hammer, a round is already chambered. Something I make sure of.

"Steve!"

My hand is jerked to the side. We swerve and grasping fingers touches my arm. A corpse flashes past.

"Where the fuck was your head?" Colette scolds. "You could have killed us!"

I guide the hammer back to rest, flip the safety on, and holster the weapon. The wind tries to take my words away. "Sorry, my mind wandered."

"Well, don't let it happen again." She lets go of my arm. "You could have killed us both and we'd be no use to anyone lying on the side of the road. I'm not going out like that."

"Sorry, hear you on that one." I shake my head, let the cobwebs go, and glance in my side view. Jeb is ten metres behind us with Mark. We need to get in and out. I slow as we approach Bloomington. This was one of those high accident intersections. People would forget to slow down when the red signal flashed and many of them died because of a truck or sleeping driver. You can't fix stupid.

I come to a stop at the lights, stare at them for a second. Nothing. Jeb stops beside me and lifts his visor. "What's up?"

The man is nice enough. Probably a middle exec or something. At least he has all his teeth for someone over forty. I shake my head. "Nothing. Just wanted to stop and take a good look. This'll probably be the last time we go into Stouffville."

"Probably not," he says, turning to glance at Mark. "You okay back there?"

The man just pats his buddy on the helmet using the bolt cutters. Not much of a talker.

"Let's get going," I say. "Faster we get in and out, the faster we're finished."

I tap the bike into gear and throttle through the intersection. No need to worry about traffic. Not now, not ever.

We pass the Gallucci Winery. A few cars are parked there and movement in the vineyard almost makes it seem as if people are picking grapes. Timber Creek is next, not the same since a new

14

company took it over in 2017, but still a fun date if you have someone you want to make laugh. I turn onto Millard and start dodging corpses. Didn't think there would be this many here. Shouldn't they all be heading north by now, migrating like last year?

"What the hell are you doing?" Colette says.

"Didn't think there'd be so many on this street. Don't worry, just need to get around a few of them."

I make a sharp turn onto Sandiford and head south. Main Street is just ahead, and from there it's only two blocks down to the town offices. A few swerves and we're through the intersection just as Jeb and Mark turn onto the street from Main. They didn't follow me. We head to the first parking lot and turn in. Not many cars are parked here, like things went to hell before anyone arrived at work, or just after they left. Four cop cars are at the back, but so far no corpses. Maybe they're in the building.

It's a one story sprawling type of building. The kind that used as much land as possible to limit the number of cars that would park there.

"Where is the gas kept?" I ask Jeb.

"Around the side of the building," he says. "They keep it there so no one will steal it." A little chuckle escapes his lips as he winks. "Like us."

We park the bikes right in front of the police cruisers and each takes a jerry can. There are two generators with a shed between them. Looks like the town wanted to be able to run no matter what. I approach the shed with Mark right behind me, jerry can in one hand and bolt cutters in the other. He's walking without a care in the world whistling a familiar tune, but hell if I could think of the name.

Colette finally smiles. "To Catch a Thief."

"What?" I look at Mark who smiles but keeps whistling.

"The song he's whistling. Big show in the sixties or something like that."

Never took Colette for a trivia person, but to each their own.

Mark is at the shed, staring at the lock. He's frowning, like someone shit in his cornflakes.

Jeb approaches. "What's wrong?"

Mark just points at the lock. Jeb jogs the rest of the way then sits down. Colette and I arrive a few seconds later to see the lock already snipped and the chain dangling from one fastener.

"Fuck," I say. I reach out and pull one of the shed doors open. Hell decides to be funny.

Skeletal hands reach out. A head, more white bone than flesh follows. The corpse is nothing more than a skeleton with flesh hanging off it. The corpse falls on Mark. He grabs at it. Bad move. The corpse snarls, mouth biting at Mark. The man doesn't scream, nothing comes out of him, not even a whimper. His eyes bulging as he pushes against the dead body, but it has more strength than I can believe.

I grab a shoulder, but flesh comes away in my hand. Now only one arm is holding Mark. He reaches into his jacket and pulls out a .45 cal hand cannon and pulls the trigger. All of us put fingers in ears too late. The racket made by firing the beast echoes through the parking lot and reaches dead ears for miles away. Bone heads must have moved. Mark doesn't. He just lays there panting. Probably deaf from the shot. We've announced ourselves to the dead.

My ears are ringing as Colette grabs my arm and says something. I see her lips flapping on her face but everything is muffled.

"What?" I scream, but she holds a hand up to her ear as well.

Mark is standing now, and I see a little wire dangling out of his jacket. He nods, smiles, and gives me the thumbs up. I shake my head and point to the wire. He makes an okay sign with a hand and attaches the wire to something behind his ear. He gives me another thumbs up.

The buzz is dying down and I can hear Colette better. "That's going to attract a lot of attention."

"I know." I push the doors aside, this time standing off centre of them. There's a second locked door with something our bolt cutters can't get though, a surface lock. Now I'm wondering what the hell we'll do. The town really blew the budget to keep gas out of the hands of looters. It hits me then. There's a line going out of the sealed area on either side. They lead to the generators. We could just tap the lines.

I wave a hand at Mark to follow the line around and point to it while making a cutting motion with my fingers. He must have figured it out. A quick cut and gas pours out of the hoses. I put my finger in the tube for lack of anything better.

"Colette, get your tank over here."

She comes over and takes the spigot out of the can. I bend the tube down and let fresh gas pour out. Gravity works wonders. The line must come out of the bottom of the tank. It starts to down out the smell of rot from the corpse.

"Do we have anything to plug this up with after we're done?" I ask.

Colette stares into the distance for a sec. "Duct tape."

"Go get some."

She runs back to the bike, rummages around for a few seconds, and sprints back holding a length of twine. "Only have this."

Jeb hands over a small knife. "Just cut it into two lengths and we'll tie them up as best we can."

Colette's can is full so I place mine under the line. Mark does the same with his as the gas spills. I look around nervously, expecting the shit to hit the fan.

The gas reaches the top of the last cans and I tie up the ends of line by pulling them through the holes, securing them higher than the fuel level. Best job yet. Mark closes the shed, putting the chain on it to secure the doors a little. He smiles and his hands make patterns in the air. He's a mute, probably went deaf at one point until he got an implant. That's what the wires are for. I'm such an idiot.

All I can do is give the man a thumbs up and we all make our way back to the bikes.

Colette glances around. "Which dealership?"

"You're kidding, right?" Jeb says. "I thought your mom told you which one."

"Shit." I put on my helmet. "Well, it's got to be the one on forty-eight. There's only five, so we look for the one without any corpses walking around and we know that's the one they cleaned out."

"And if they couldn't clean it out?" Colette asks.

"They we make our way back to the camp," I say. "Better get going, we're burning daylight."

We take off back to Main Street and across to Baker Hill, then onto Millard again. The Chrysler store is the one we hit, but there are corpses walking around inside. Most have dark tans with flesh peeling off as if in the sun too long. Don't think they went in there. We bypass the Toyota and Honda, knowing they didn't sell the types of vans we need and head to Nissan. I like their SUVs, but they wouldn't help. I shake my head.

"So, when the Ford dealership was closed five years ago—"

"The Ford dealerships didn't close," Jeb says. "They were cleared of all charges on the roll back scam."

That's it; I need to find out more before we go on a raid. "I bet that's where they are. Ford is the only one who really puts out a van for businesses, unless they went to Uxbridge."

"Or Newmarket," Colette adds.

"Let's get going."

We take it slow this time, following our path back to Main. Once busy shops now stand with parking lots partially full and no cars moving around. Fast food outlets litter the south of the road and groceries stores seem inviting, no line ups. Jeb turns into the plaza just before the Pizzaville. He pulls up to the first store and jumps off the bike. It's the liquor store. Our own little glass enclosed sin city in the small town. The man yanks open the doors and walks in. I pull up beside their bike to see Mark gazing into the store window. He just looks around and shrugs his shoulders.

Jeb is in there, a big combat knife in hand. He walks about the store and slides the knife into the base of one corpse's neck. It crumples to the ground. He moves on, not going after them all, just those in his way. At one wall display he stops. His knife flashes and the display case door opens. He grabs two bottles and closes the case. One quick turn and he's walking to the exit, two bottles in hand, a line of corpses lurching in his wake.

Colette's head hits my back. "That was stupid."

"I could never afford one of these." He holds up a bottle of rum covered in dust. "The thing is a thousand in the store, so I figured it'd be a good investment now the world's gone to shit." He tosses a bottle to me. "Paulette said you liked the stuff, too, so I got you a bottle."

A gun shot rings out and I almost drop the precious liquid. "Did you hear where that came from?" I ask Collette.

"No."

"The dealership!" Jeb exclaims.

We both hit the gas and ride over to the other building with the big FORD sign in front. I don't know what to expect but if someone is shooting, we're going to have a lot of company very soon – the kind who have you for dinner.

3

NEW

The dealership is only sixty-odd metres away, so it takes little time to get there. Corpses stagger toward it; odd lumbering bodies of decomposing flesh. Some of them still resemble the people they were, but with a bluish tint. Most have decomposed exposing bone and rotting muscle. A few have rips across their middle as if something tried to eat them before they started to walk.

They converge on the place from the east, likely the earlier shot woke them up. But the smell they bring almost makes me gag. Old rotten chicken left in the sun for a few days is mild compared to the stench. The population of Stouffville exploded over the last couple of years, but the true mass of dead takes me aback. More wasted humanity walks the street now than before. Even when Mindy and I came into the town last year we didn't see so many.

It must be the migration. The strange action they are taking travelling North for the summer and South for the winter. Like a flock of destitute crows seeking anything to eat. A large group of about fifty corpses stumble toward us on shaking legs. And, just like ants, you can take out a few but eventually a mob of them will get you.

We could out run them, but we needed to get the gas to the other survivors in the dealership. No hesitation involved, just a quick turn of the grip. The bike shoots forward and through the grass separating the two parking lots. I dodge between a few parked cars. Colette tightens her hold on me while we weave. It's hard to breath with her squeezing so tight.

My side view mirror reveals Jeb keeping up with me, Mark hangs on with only one arm and points to something quickly. There's no way of telling at what for his hand goes back to holding his nose.

Colette shoots out an arm. She makes a sweeping motion trying to get me to go around the dealership and approach from behind. I get it, finally. I head us off into that direction, leading the lumbering bodies.

Around into the repair area, the back lot is just about empty. A sign of economic boom. Low inventory usually means high car sales. One of the roll-up doors is open and a guy is there waving at us. Hell, open invitation if I ever saw one. A quick lean gets us in line with the place and through the opening. I take the pressure off the throttle and slow to a stop where Charlie and some other guy are under the hood of a large cargo van. The thing is big and boxy. Basically perfect for our needs. The two argue in hushed tones and gesture wildly, so I keep away. Colette walks right over to them, peering over their shoulders.

Jeb comes to a stop beside me, smile on his face, as Mark lets go. I can see something brewing behind those blue eyes but I dare not ask.

"Hell is empty. And all the devils are here," he says in a terrible British accent.

"What?" I don't understand the reference.

"Shakespeare, from The Tempest. Didn't you study it in school?" Jeb shakes his head. "They don't teach kids nothing these days."

"Didn't take much Shakespeare when I went to school. Computer geek, remember." I put the kick stand down and climb off the bike. "Anyway, we just made it here in time. Did you see that horde?"

Mark pulls off his helmet and nods. His hands weave an intricate pattern while Jeb and I watch.

"He thinks you need to learn how to drive better." Jeb signs back. He's talking to Mark about me, why else use something I can't understand. They both laugh.

"Out with it," I demand.

"Mark wants to know who taught you how to ride? A chimp or

something? At least you shoot better than you ride or we'd all be in trouble."

"Funny." I glance around the shop. Three bays are empty and the others have cars, besides the one with the van in it. Seems like the place was hopping when hell broke loose. "Who shot what?"

The guy who handled the garage door walks over from the entrance. He's younger than Jeb, maybe by about ten years or so. That's not saying much for I haven't figured out how old Jeb is yet. Somewhere between fifty and seventy I would say. His skin is wrinkled but eyes are sharp, and he's old-guy strong. Bet he works in the sun all the time.

The younger man holds out his hand. "We haven't met. My name's Stan."

I take the hand. He's got a hell of a grip. "Steve. Pleasure to meet you, Stan."

"Jeb get into the liquor store this trip?"

"Sure did!" Jeb holds out his bottle. "Good snatch this time."

"Damn! We share a place and he's a loud drunk."

"Sorry about that," I say. "Could be worse."

"Really?"

"He could snore."

Stan lets out a soft bark. "He does. And louder when he's been drinking."

"Sorry."

Stan points to the van. "We're lucky this one was in the spot when we got here."

"Who shot their gun?" I ask.

"Charlie. He's such a lousy shot, too. Should never have given the thing to him but he insisted. Wanted to have protection." Stan guides me to the side and out of the way of the rest of the group. "Your girl, Colette is it?"

"Yes," I say. "But she's not my girl, just a friend."

"Oh." It sounds like he's apologizing.

"She's married."

His eyes widen. "Really? Where's the man?"

"Part of the group we need to rescue."

"Oh, well, I guess that's okay." He takes a few steps toward the van. "You may have noticed a lack of women at the lake." He scratches his head. "Wouldn't mind finding someone to be with while we wait this crap-hole world out."

"I get you on that one." I glance at the three people crowded around the van's hood. "What's the hold up?"

Charlie stands back with a frown. "Stupid thing won't start."

"Could that be the reason it's in here?" I glance over to the roll-up door. A lot of heads are moving past the cut out windows.

Colette steps away from the van. She sighs and rubs her nose, a small dirt stain now decorates the small button in the middle of her face. "No, it's here for a simple inspection before delivery, according to the paperwork."

A few heads move past the front doors. The corpses are assembling and we're all in one place. I step out of their sight. More bodies means trouble getting out. A sniff tells me lots of the rotten bodies are piling up outside. If they do make their way into the garage, we'll need to have more weapons then we have right now. Something tells me this day isn't turning out the way we want it to.

Mark wanders over to the van, opens the driver's door, and sticks his head under the dash. A few seconds pass as he fiddles with something, then he pulls himself onto the driver's seat and turns the ignition. The engine struggles to turn over.

Charlie bangs his head on the hood. Colette jumps back. The third guy I don't know, but he dashes back so fast he bumps into the tool case. The tray bounces. Metal hits metal. Mark just smiles in the van. I glance to the roll-up door and the corpses getting more animated.

"What the fuck?" Charlie rushes over to the driver's side and pulls open the door. "Fuck! What'd you do, Mark?"

Mark starts to sign and then stops.

Jeb walks toward the group. "Charlie doesn't know sign language. Mark just told him he's stupider than a stump."

"Jeb, tell Mark to get out of the van," Charlie says.

"Mark, get out of the van." Jeb smiles. "Just because he can't speak doesn't mean he's stupid or can't hear." Jeb taps his ear. "Remember, he has an implant."

Charlie blushes. "No offence, ya' just surprised me, that's all."

"Shit your pants more like it." Colette frowns, pushes a few stray hairs out of her eyes. "Just like me. What'd you do, Mark?"

The man signs at a frantic pace, fingers flying. Jeb starts to laugh. "A kill switch. They installed it under the dash just like other vans on the lot."

Colette hikes up her pants a little. "And how did you figure that one out, Mark?"

Jeb nods and turns to us. "Because he drove one just like it for Pet Value before the world went to shit."

───

Charlie takes his time carefully putting things back together on the van. Jeb and I empty the jerry cans into the tank. The needle on the gas gauge comes to rest just under half-full. At least that went well. Mark stands to the side with a slight smile and the knowledge he helped once again. Colette is hunting for something around the shop, sticking her head into one vehicle and then the next. She lets out a big "Ah ha!" and rushes back to me.

There's a huge triumphant smile on her face. "I found it!"

"Found what?" What the hell was she looking for?

"Something for Zoey." She holds out her hand and laying there is a plastic toy lady bug. "Not sure what it does, but there's room for batteries and everything."

"And what's she going to do with that?"

"I just thought–"

Charlie starts up the van. The engine catches, coughs, then roars to life. He slams the steering wheel. "Yes!"

"We can put the bikes in the back and all climb in," he yells.

Banging starts up on the other side of the roll-up door. I image corpses pressing against it from the noise. "Keep your voice down."

His cheeks redden. "Sorry."

"I'll take the bike back," I say.

Colette stares at the men for a second then shakes her head. "I'm going with Steve."

Both Jeb and Mark agree they'll ride back to the camp. One big happy family making their way home again.

I climb on the bike. "I'll get the door."

Colette gets on behind me, and we ride the short distance to the garage exit. Usually, a small motor pulls the roll-up, but there's no power. I reach for the chain and haul on it. A small sliver of light spills through the bottom. This is going to take a while. I give a good ten pulls to move the thing up a few centimetres, and when it's up less than a foot, Colette grabs the chain to stop it. I'm just watching the door and give the thing a good yank, making Colette yelp. She swats me on the back of the head.

"You have to start looking around!" She points at the bottom of the door. More importantly, she's pointing at the dirty shoes shuffling back and forth in front of it. There's a horde outside waiting for me to finish ringing the dinner bell to the all night buffet. There are so many corpses their legs block out most of the light. I wave for Charlie to bring the van to the door. It's not big enough to block the entrance so I get him to turn around. With a little care, we have the back of the vehicle blocking most of the way near the chain. At least we'll be safe. But it will leave a huge gap at the other side.

Jeb and Mark sit on their bike just in front of the van, waiting for an opening to gun it.

"When the door is up enough, I'll let you know. Get through the door and out of the way fast, we'll need the room to get up to speed and free of the groping hands," I tell Charlie.

He nods.

I start yanking on the chain again. It's slow going, but at least the corpses can't get at me. It's a good plan, but I see the milky eyes of the dead through the crack as the door goes up and I stop hauling for a second. Fetid breath floats through the opening and I gag. Fingers find their way between the door and truck searching for a way in. My heart hammers as they try to push against the opening, tearing skin away from muscle and bone in an attempt to reach me.

By the time the door is at the roof of the van, corpses are squeezing past the driver's side and falling into the garage. There's one or two under the van as well, I call them crawlers. They can be the most dangerous. They move under everything in their relentless pursuit of flesh. Nothing's wrong with their legs; they use them to propel forward at a good speed. It's just they don't stand up. Whether it has to do with intelligence or balance, I don't know. Once they have fallen, they don't stop to stand again. Nothing in their minds tells them to do so and that means they crawl the rest of the time. It makes for a shorter time they can move for their bodies get moist fast and they don't feel the ground grating away at their skin. This rips them open and soon they're dragging entrails behind them. Sometimes the birds take advantage of the exposed flesh. Especially the crows.

They remind me of the boogeyman hidden under the bed ready to grab your leg.

The van guns through the door, taking bodies upon bodies with it. There's more of them outside than I thought. They appear to congregate around the ones moving, following them, hoping for a good snack or something. Too many for us to get through, but Jeb tries anyway. He stays in the wake of the van for a few metres before they run out of space. Then he makes a race for the road.

The corpses are slow, but single minded. They close ranks and dirty, rotten hands grab at the two. Mark falls off the back as Jeb guns the bike enough for it to do a wheelie. The man has no voice, which makes what I see that much more terrifying. Hands reach down, pulling at clothes until they rip off. Sharp fingers reach and grasp flesh, pulling it away from muscle and bone. Blood erupts from the wounds and then we are cut off from seeing any more because of the tide of bodies descending on our companion.

Colette shakes, but I have no time to be nice about what's happening . If they're lucky, the corpses will completely devour them. If not, they'll turn just like everyone else.

I reach out and yank the chain the other way and the door comes down with agonizingly slow chugs. It's taking too long. I give the chain one big pull and jump onto the bike. Colette follows. Gunning the engine, I take us into the garage.

The door to the Showroom is unlocked and the front tire hits it just hard enough to push it open. There's no way the door's going to hold back the horde. Inside are a few vehicles with stickers on them bragging gas mileage and other safety features. I see movement, but it's outside, not in. A quick jerk of the handles makes us face to the west exit and the bike responds to my commands. Out of the mirror I spy Jeb's bike covered with corpses. Hands are pulling flesh from his body. His eyes stare at the sky, lips parted in a never ending scream as corpses grab entrails and stuff them into waiting mouths. Blood no longer flows out of his body.

Only a few corpses block the west exit. The van lumbers through the east part of the lot making a ton of noise and pushing corpse after corpse under its wheels. We stop at the door just as a body lumbers up to it. The thing leans on the door and bangs against the glass with surprising speed. It must be a fresh one, but from where? Could be Markham. It hits the glass again but not very hard, but if it keeps hammering, the doorway will be crawling with corpses in no time. Once enough of them are there, the glass will shatter from the weight and we'll be done for.

I take out my Glock, aim it between the eyes of the corpse, and pull the trigger. The weapon barks. Glass shatters. The corpse collapses. I hit the throttle and we rocket through the door, tire slipping on the tiles. The back-end slides. Front tire hits the body and bounces. The handle bars jerk. Then the back end bucks and the handles jar to the side as I struggle with the bike. Wrench the grips to the left, then right. Lean, but too fast for Colette. On my way back she's still going the wrong way. Her hands grasp hard against me. She starts to lose balance. I lean back again, turn the bike right instead of left but the rear end slides too much and then bites into the pavement. The bike stops sliding. Our inertia keeps us going. A pickup is right there and we slam into it.

We hit the truck. Colette's grip loosens. The bike goes out from under me and flips. I keep my feet. Colette lands on her back. She starts wheezing. Air knocked out. Got to get her to her feet. I reach down, grab her hand. A tug and she's up but then doubles over. I pull off her helmet and she barfs. My stomach rolls. The smell of bile underlies that of rotting flesh. Never could stand that smell. I lean her against the truck, corpses walking toward us. The bike is right there. We need to get on going, *now*.

I grasp the handle bars of the bike and yank. It's heavier than I think. But once up, I look at Colette, she's almost caught her breath. She's a trooper. One leg is over the seat and both hands clasp around me. I twist the throttle and we hop the curb onto Main Street. In less than a minute we're on forty-eight and heading north. I let us slow down to a reasonable sixty and lift my visor.

"You okay?" I yell back to her.

"Yeah, but my side hurts." She leans to the left. "Can we stop for a sec."

I slow down and stop. Colette steps off and bends over with her hand against her left side. Her pants are a little wet and I glance over to the saddle bag. It's dripping. The bottle is smashed, that's the only thing I can think happened.

This outing cost us two lives.

With a world gone to hell, it's not something we can afford to have happen. I run the numbers like only a geek can. Analytically, we're going to save five to ten people. Already two are dead on our side. If we lose any more the number of lives we rescue will not be even to the ones we lose. But then again, if the bikers are left to their own devices, they'll soon be in the Muscleman Lake area and threatening our new home. The lives would have been lost anyway. No, the logic doesn't add up. Nowhere close.

Life. It all comes down to that. We could lose the fight to get my people back. To get Mindy back. Will it be worth it for them to sacrifice themselves for people they don't know?

Colette stands tall, hand still on her side. She takes a few steps toward me and I look down the highway. Cars are all over the place. I don't remember them. We are alive. A glance north shows more of the same. Cars all over.

I don't want to take Bloomington into the lake area. Too many corpses could follow us. Lakeshore Road should be good. We'll go through the new development. Follow the old hydro line through the forest. Just have to remember to weave around the poles until we get to the camp.

"Is it worth it?" I ask Colette.

"What?" She looks at me with a raised eyebrow.

"All we're going through. Is it worth it?"

She nods. "Sure is." A deep breath and she straightens up. "Do you want to give up?"

There's no way I'm giving up until Mindy is by my side. "No."

A squirrel runs to the side of the road, looks at us, scampers forward until he's about five metres away and stands on his hind legs sniffing the air.

"You don't sound too convincing."

The squirrel's head turns sideways, ears perking up.

"I need Mindy back." Her in the hands of Pa runs through my mind. Heat builds in my cheeks.

A bushy tail goes erect and waves behind it. Its mouth opens and a "kuk" sound repeats.

"I just thought – Shit!" Colette screams.

The squirrel flattens, then scurries off the way it came. I turn to Colette ready to ask what's happening. She's yanking her arm away from a rotted-toothed corpse.

4

PUSHING DAISIES

I step toward Colette, bring up my helmet, and smash it into the corpse's head. Colette pulls her arm free as the no-longer-animated corpse crumples to the ground, spraying sludge like liquid. Black blood from the attacker covers the hand she must have had against its forehead to help stave off the bite.

There are more behind it, all lumbering out of the brush. We can take some of them out, but not all. It's time to go. The guys should be at the Lafarge pit south of the lake by now, storing the vehicle. I glance at the sky, still early but the afternoon rising. Time to get back to the camp.

"You good to go?" I ask Colette.

She's shaky, eyes a little wide, but not totally out to lunch. I'm impressed, she's gone from a simple girl who married young to a much stronger woman. Almost as strong as Mindy.

"Colette, we need to get out of here." I point at corpses now only a few metres away. It's like they're drawn to us, as if smelling a meal after starving for so long.

We need to move.

Now.

"Yes… Right." She shakes off the stupor, looks around as if trying to get her bearings, and stares at the sea of dead coming from the forest. "Strange." One hand comes up and runs through her hair. "Why are there so many in the forest?"

"Let's worry about that later." I mount the bike and put the kick-stand back. "Come on, Colette, let's get out of here."

She climbs on the back of the bike, voice full of wonder. "You think they're still alive?"

"They better be." Three corpses converge on us, their arms out and fingers grasping. "If they're not, the two of us are going on a hunting spree."

Her arms encircle my waist, head leaning against my back. I twist the accelerator and barely hear her say, "Yes, we will."

Trees zip past as I drive down the gravel road. I don't stop until we're in front of Mom's house. I'm out of breath, heart pounding. There were too many close calls on this outing, and too many deaths.

The screen door of Mom's house slams shut. Zoey runs outside and into Colette's arms, laughing. She's dusted with a little flour in her hair and chocolate smears her cheek. It's an interesting sight. Too bad I don't have a camera; memories like this need to be saved.

Zoey releases Colette and runs to me, little arms encircle my legs, and she barriers her face into my thigh. I place a hand on her head, taking a second to bask in the child's love. Another thing to fight for, to strive for survival.

I extract myself from her grasp and kneel down. "Someone may have something for you."

The door opens and Mom comes out wiping her hands on a dish cloth. I think she's been baking with Zoey and that could mean a cake or something. Mom must be getting soft in her old age.

She steps to the edge of the veranda and nods. "How did it go?"

I drop my head. This is the question I don't want to answer. Losing people in just the setup is bad. We're down two who possessed certain abilities, like thinking outside the box. I just shake my head and walk to the house. There's nothing I can really say.

As I step onto the veranda, Mom takes my arm and stares into my eyes. I stare back, not looking away. There's a want to ask a question deep within those orbs, but also a dread at what the answer may be.

"Not here." I look over at Zoey. "Inside and away from sensitive ears."

Mom understands and lets go. I walk inside the house and head toward the living room. The aroma of rich dark chocolate wafts from the kitchen. Who knows where it came from.

I sit on the couch and Mom sits beside me. She doesn't look at me or offer a hand to squeeze. "What's wrong?"

Zoey squeals with delight outside. I take a deep breath, hold it, and let it out slow. There's no way around it, she deserves to hear what happened and now. If I wait for the others to come back then we'll get into an argument. Not a good thing to do with someone who interrogated a lot of very bad people in her lifetime.

"We lost Jeb and Mike." There, it's out. I take a deep breath hoping it will slow my hammering heart.

"What happened?"

A level question. There's no blame in it, just a simple little request for information that I have. So I tell her. Everything. From getting the gas to being given a bottle of rum. When I get to the gun shot at the town hall she just stares. Then I go right on to the van and getting it out of the dealership. I expect her to start asking questions as I describe the incident of Jeb and Mark's death. Mom rubs her eyes and I see moisture. She didn't even cry when Dad died, so why the hell is she letting go now?

"So, Jeb is dead." She puts her hands together and presses them to her lips as if praying. "I guess that ends it. Unless you think…"

"No, there were too many corpses around to get away. The bike went down and before our view was obscured I saw what they did. If he lived longer than a minute I'd be surprised."

"It must have been painful."

There's another tear. "I would think he died fast from the blood loss."

She nods, wipes at her eyes. "Well, that settles it."

I stare at nothing while Mom walks into the kitchen. Dishes move about. Plates clink together. A tray hits the floor. Grief in the form of soft crying comes from the kitchen.

Something's not right. I get up and make my way to Mom, not sure what's going on. What I see is strange. Mom is sitting on the floor, tray lying beside her, brownie slab shattered in front of her. I watch her shoulders rise and fall. Tears find routes around the hands that cup her face. I've never seen her like this. The strongest woman I know is breaking down in front of me. I don't understand what's happening. She wasn't like this when Dad died. If she shed a tear for him I never saw it. But Jeb and Mike's death has made her into a blubbering mess.

I don't want the others to see her like this. Hell, I don't want to see her like this. She's been the cement that's held these people together and it may not bode well if they see her falling apart, let alone the gut tightening sensation it's making me feel.

A few steps and I'm beside her. Down to one knee I go. Gently place an arm around her and then she's pulling me to her. I let it happen. Offer what little strength I have to help comfort her. We stay in this position, neither of us letting go. Grief needs to be released, and something tells me she's been holding on to it for a long time.

But like all good things, I know it has to come to an end. As her fingers loosen, I pull away. Her eyes are a little puffy from the tears and she wipes away the evidence of what happened. A quick sniffle and she closes her eyes, straightens her back, and stands, brushing off evidence of what happened.

We clean up the mess in silence. The brownies we cannot rescue so it is my duty to whip up another batch so Zoey doesn't know what happened. I don't need to have a hysterical child on my hands. So, beating eggs and adding flour from the dwindling supplies is my duty. Mom hands me the baker's chocolate and some purple sugar. Beet sugar. That's how she's been doing it. Probably has them growing in a field somewhere. I get the tray into the oven and go over to the kitchen table where Mom sits. She lights a cigarette, takes a puff, coughs, and snubs the thing out. I haven't seen her smoke in years, and the way she reacted, it's been years since she last did.

"Take these stale things away, will you?" She tosses a pack of Camels to me.

I frown. Written on the package is the date 2010, the date I bought her that last package of cigarettes. Twelve years. No wonder she coughed.

"This was the last pack, right?"

"Filthy habit." She takes the ashtray and throws it out the back door. As she comes back, some of her colour returns. "Jeb and I"–her lower lip trembles–"we'd been seeing each other for a couple of years."

All emotion is gone now from her voice and we're back to being just two people who know each other.

"I didn't know."

"We kept it quiet for a while. Didn't want anything to interrupt the business. He invested in the camp during the shit years of the liberal party. Then, when the world went to hell he moved in and the people who followed were the ones who made it past the first month. Nothing special, just people who didn't get bit."

"How many?"

"I didn't teach you to be vague, Steven. How many what?"

"People. I only saw a few of them yesterday when we planned the raid. How many do you have in the camp?"

She gazes into my eyes for a few seconds. It's like a game to her, how much information should she give me and when. It's all in the training I got really tired of it when I grew up. That's why I left. She must think now is about the right time.

"About fifty scattered about and in the forest area."

I must have looked funny with my mouth open.

She smiles. "Yes, we have a lot of little cabins in the woods south of the lake now. Most people grabbed what they could from the mobile home places and drove them until they stopped." Her smile disappears. "Took us a while to figure out the bikers would spot some stuff from the road and take advantage of people so we made sure no one would see them."

The drone of a plane's engine sounds in the distance. Not a jet, one of those prop ones.

Mom tilts her head, then her eyes go wide. "Do you know anyone who can fly a plane?"

Over a dozen people stand in the field, one or both hands shielding their eyes as they look up at the sky and watch the bi-plane do a lazy circle of the area. The light drone of the engine drifts down to us and offers a small distraction from the birds. One of the group has a white blanket out as if to signal, but the rest of us get her to put it aside.

It's been a long time since I flew a plane, but with the double wings it's probably a crop duster and can fly slow and low. Don't know if there's enough room for it to land but if it does, who the hell would be piloting it?

The plane heads north over the pond at about one hundred metres and wing wags as it passes. The trees north of the pond swallow it up and the engine drones into the distance. The noise comes back. This time the plane comes right toward us, just missing the tree tops. The pilot flies over the repair shed at eight metres off the ground and once past it, drops to the ground in the dirt parking lot. We scatter.

Dust flies through the air as the pilot cuts the throttle. The thing bounces a little, then the tail hits the ground. It keeps slowing until fifty metres is eaten away and engine is gunned a little. The plane rolls up to Mom's house and stops. The engine sputters a little and the prop finally ceases spinning. Everyone rushes to the plane as if it's the last chicken dinner on Earth.

By the time we get to the plane, the pilot is out and pushing against the tail to swing it around. Funniest thing I've seen in a while. This person really looked the part. An old leather flying cap sat on a strangely shaped head and goggles still covered his eyes. Not big, not even built well. This skinny man just pushed. And when I reached him, the first thing I notice is he is not a he, he's a she. Blonde hair sticks out haphazardly from under the cap and she sports the brightest rogue and lipstick I've ever seen. Her leather jacket could hardly zip up due to ample breasts. Everything looks worn on her, from the leathers to the tan pants.

I don't really care where she came from, just that she has a plane and can get us where we want to go fast. A plan starts to form in my mind.

She looks over at me and smiles. "Could you give a girl a hand?"

Maybe it was the smile or maybe the lilt of her light British accent that gets me, but I come up beside her and help push until the plane is pointed north again and ready for take-off.

"That's marvellous. My name's Danielle, Danny for short. I hate to ask but… do you happen to have a loo I could use?"

It takes only a few minutes for Danny to finish what she needed to do and return from the outhouse by the lake. Mom gives me one of those looks telling me to be cautious around her until we understand what's going on. That means no access to anything that will lead her to knowing how well-off, or bad-off, we are.

She walks toward us with a smile on her face and a piece of toilet paper in hand. Her smile beams across the whole gathering and she holds up the piece of ply. "Civilization!" A bunch of us laugh.

"Really, you have to understand what it's like," she says to me. "I've been flying all over trying to find people who are civilized and nice. One group shot at me, another seemed to be eating well but as I started to land I noticed why. I abandoned my landing, not wanting to be the next person for dinner, literally. Others just rush at me with weapons raised like I'm the devil himself." She scans the faces again. "Your group is the only one that actually just came out to watch. And when you came running, none of you held a weapon or a shank of leg or something."

I just nod. We need to let her talk. This way Mom can take mental notes and figure out what this person's deal is. Just keep her talking.

"Where'd you come from?" I ask, a good question. Find out her base and work forward to now.

"Oh, I flew down here from the Kawartha's, Kirkfield to be proper." She keeps smiling. "Been lengthening my search for people every day since the problems started last year."

I take an off-script stab at a question. "How far have you been?"

She thinks for a while, eyes staring off into the distance. "Went up to Washago, nothing there. Orillia is just the infected walking around. Barrie is in bad shape, lots of fires over the last few months. Your town south of here looked lively but it's just corpses moving about. Did see a big van drive off from there and that's what I followed until it went into the bushes just south of you. Then I flew over you guys." She glances at all the faces. "Are you all related?"

Mom chuckles this time. "No, we don't inbreed here. The town is small, but we're all from different stock, except him." She indicates me with her chin. "He's my boy."

"Oh, bravo." Danny gives me a winning smile.

I see Mindy in that smile somehow, and my heart falls. This woman is nothing like Mindy. She's taller, a little over weight, older, very different.

Danny frowns at my reaction. "Did I say something wrong?"

Mom comes up and takes Danny's arm. "No. A couple of towns over, a biker gang is playing havoc in the area and kidnapped a whole community of people. We're in the process of getting them back and" –she turns her head toward the plane– "you've came at the right time to help out."

Danny listens to Mom explain everything. She listens attentively and asks questions at the right times, staying silent at the others.

Mom now has a good plan to get everyone back. It depends on a number of things going right for us, and this time I really hope we can pull it off. Getting the guys with the van back to camp helped boost the moral a bit. Heck, we lost two on the little trip into Stouffville, just imagine what would happen if we tried to pull off a rescue without getting things down solid.

I take a small group with me to the gun club area in Uxbridge. The bikers haven't been there for a while, we can tell. The doors to the main clubhouse are torn off but the office is still in one piece as well as the vault. We raid the stash of guns and ammo, making sure to close and lock the safe the way we did before. Now we're armed.

Mom and a bunch of people cook up some really nice surprises, and Zoey gets some treats as well. It seems the women in the area are mostly farmers and know how to pull toffee and roll salty sugar bombs. The child is running around outside right now with a few other kids trying to burn off the excess energy.

Danny likes the way we think here, especially since we're planning to rescue our own against certain death or slavery. She's in with us more than I would have guessed.

We finished all our preparations and load the surprise into the plane. Danny is certain she has enough room to take-off, but I pace it out and push the plane right up against the side of the house to make sure.

I check her fuel – she has over half a tank. More than enough for the little run she's about to do. Good thing the plane is old, we can put crappy gas in it and it'll run. Danny says they just knew how to make engines back then. I know it's because there's no computers or emission stuff on it. Say what you will, but now there's only a few of us and a little CO_2 isn't going to hurt anyone in this world of ours now.

We check our watches, verify they're all on the same time, and head out. I'm in the truck with Charlie; Colette is stuck minding Zoey. It's the fourth day since we arrived and everyone is following our lead. We have five people in the back of the van to help others if needed and I'm loaded to bear with two scoped out rifles and a compound bow.

It's time to get our people and say hello to The Family.

5

IS IT ME YOU'RE LOOKING FOR?

Charlie and I start talking about sausages. Not the kind you eat. It's something I heard a long time ago, when people make small talk because they don't like the silence. Just like talking about the weather but not really talking about it. I find out he played World of Warcraft. It takes a while, but he starts telling me about his character and all the stuff he accumulated in the game. It ends up he believes people died because they just didn't know how to survive. He says if it wasn't for Jeb and knowing Mom, he never would have made it.

We drive down Ninth Line to Bloomington, turn east and go until we hit Goodwood Road and then Concession seven. A left turn takes us to the Miller Asphalt Plant and the first of many pits to check out. The radio on the dash throws static. I'm waiting for Danny to get over the pit and tell us if there's anyone trapped. Probably just corpses milling about. I don't doubt the family corralled as many as they could in the pits surrounding the area. It makes sense if you ask me, just get them to follow something and there you go. Instant corpse cage.

The drone of Danny's plane comes from the north. She's already done part of her job. We talked about it, wanting to make sure The Family didn't come back to where we stationed ourselves. Danny's job was to fly north, then east. She would come into the town from the northeast and Mom would drop some M4's, quarter sticks of dynamite, out of the plane as they flew over, then start flying northeast again. They would drop a bunch of caltrops on the roads they pass just to slow down the groups who try to follow. Once out of sight, they would drop to twenty metres and make their way to the first pit, this pit. A little scouting and we'll know if our people are here or not. Then they'll go to the next pit and so on. This should cut the search time.

The radio comes to life. "Nothing in that pit. No raised area, just corpses moving about."

It was Mom. I grab the radio and key the mic. "Everything good up there?"

"Little windy for my taste. Should have worn a heavier jacket. It's cold."

"Guess you'll listen to me next time." I give a little smile. "Check out the Van Camp pits off Lake Ridge and then the Lafarge one off seven. We should be ready when you're able to report in."

"On our way," she says and keys off the mic.

"Where're we going from here?" Charlie asks.

"South. It'd be easier to hit the Lafarge site and double up to the others."

"Sounds good." He puts the truck into gear and turns around. "Never knew there were so many pits around here. We counted ten when we drew the plan."

The truck bumps against something and I see a decomposed hand drop out of view. Charlie smiles.

"Total of sixteen in the area, not counting the ones they closed down and built little communities on." I count in my head. "Three sites converted to those estate homes, you know, the ones worth more than two million each."

Charlie just whistles and pulls away from the corpse crushed against a post. "Good deed for the day, there."

The back of the van bangs. "You guys be careful. There's no seats back here."

"Sounds like Larry doesn't like being in the back with those two other guys. Maybe if we hit a few pot holes he'd be nicer to us." To illustrate his point, Charlie starts to weave a little, hitting the pot holes in the road.

The world is getting rid of the human experience. In just over two hundred years we paved kilometre after kilometre of road, and now plants are jutting out of cracks, pushing the pavement farther apart than ever. Makes for more chances of infestation for wildlife. It reminds me we have to start planting soon. Mindy confessed to loving this time of year. Spring, when everything starts to bloom again. And then it hits me. Mindy, I really need to find her.

As if reading my mind, or maybe my expression, Charlie swerves, misses a corpse and asks, "So, tell me about Mindy."

"What you want to know?"

"How did you meet her?"

I think back to that day and her banging on the server room door, the dead rushing toward us. The tale fills the time between pits. He listens to me pour out thoughts of her and what makes me want to find her. Finally, as we pass the burnt out shell that was my home a lifetime ago, I finish by explaining that she's pregnant.

"We'll find her," he says.

We get to the Lafarge gravel pit at the same time as the plane. Mom's voice cracks over the radio. "The Van Camp pit has some people on a raised area. Looks like a steep ramp and the van will need a running start, but the place is covered with corpses."

"Copy that," I say. "Was it the east or west one?"

"East one."

"Good. I have a plan for that one." I wink at Charlie. "What about this pit?"

"Passing over now."

We watch the sky as the plane flies overhead. I grip the steering wheel hoping there's something here.

"Nothing but corpses."

I key the mic. "This would be a great pit for it. Lafarge always digs deep, sometimes to the water table."

"Nope, only corpses milling about. I can't see– Wait, found something."

We watch as the plane circles and drops lower. They must be ten metres off the ground. Not safe but great for getting a better look.

Gunfire erupts from the pit and I pull out my Glock.

"Shit! Someone's down there on a freight box waving hands. Looks like a girl from what I can see," Mom yells over the radio.

I take a deep breath and hold.

"You said Mindy was Asian?" Mom's voice is excited.

"Yes, Chinese," I say, almost forgetting to key the mic.

"She's what, about four months along?"

"More like six, but hard to tell because she's so small."

Charlie is smiling. It's like he's feeding off my excitement.

"We have a small, Asian, pregnant female standing on a cargo container waving her hands. I see a lot of corpses so you'll need to either run them over or push them out of the way."

I stare at the pit, stomach rolling. The corpses are all around the container, blocking off the best approach. Probably because the land is flat. Mom guides us up to the spot and Charlie comes right beside the container, pushing the corpses out of the way or running them over. He turns on the air to clear the stench only to have it intensify. With a quick twist, I turn it off.

He's not going fast so most corpses are just pushed over to crawl the rest of their existence away. My heart sinks as we approach. I can tell right away. It's not Mindy. Too much to ask the universe to be kind to us. But it is a young girl, maybe fifteen, and she's Chinese, and pregnant. Someone who needs rescuing.

As we pull up, she jumps onto the roof of the van and scrambles to the edge. She's dirty, sweaty, and really ragged with ripped pants and shirt. I roll down the window quick, just enough to pass her some water. It's snatched from my hand.

"Thanks," she says and wipes her mouth with a shaking hand. "There's people in the container."

"Damn," Charlie says. "How the hell do we get them out?"

A problem. Something to work on instead of worrying about Mindy. I welcome it, dissect it, throw it through the grinder known as my mind, and spit out a resolution.

"Charlie, can you back right up to the container?" I ask.

"Sure, but what–"

"No time." I glance up at the teenager. "Go to the back and when we're right up against the opening hammer against the roof as hard as you can."

Her eyes don't blink for a second. "Back out there?"

"That's the hardest part." I roll the window down half-way. The stink of rotting flesh fills the cabin and I gag. No time to worry about it. I adjust the mirror. "Can you do it?"

"Yeah, I can do it."

"Line us up as best you can with the cargo opening. Back up until the girl taps the top and we'll be right on it." I hammer the back wall of the cab. "Larry," I yell.

"Yeah?" His voice is muffled, but still loud enough. Hopefully he can hear me.

"We're backing up to a rail car container. When I give the signal, roll up the door and see if you can open it up. There's going to be someone on the roof directing us, so when you hear something there, ignore it."

"Yeah, thought I heard something up there." I strain to pick up his voice. "Okay, you heard the guy."

He fades away to incoherent mutters as we start backing up. The buzzer on the cargo van makes a lot of noise but we're okay. Charlie is backing up slow, enough to get us there but not enough to bump us into anything. When the hammering on the roof starts we bump against the container. Close.

I hammer against the back wall of the cab. "Now!"

The back rolls up. The sound echoing through the whole van gives me hope. We wait for the report. Something needs to be done soon; the crowd of corpses grows thick around the van.

"We need to move," Charlie says reading my mind. "There may be too many of them to get through. Hope they don't clog up the intakes."

"Move forward a few feet real slow," the teen on the roof yells.

Charlie puts the van into gear and crawls forward. At a metre the girl bangs on the roof. "Stop!"

We wait for another agonizing few minutes.

"What's going on there?" Mom shrieks over the radio.

"It wasn't Mindy, but there're some people in the container that we're getting out."

"Well, hurry up," Mom says, her voice sharp. "You got a whole bunch of corpses coming out of the forest to the north."

I look out Charlie's window and see the line moving forward. Just a blur right now for they're about a hundred metres away, but it's impressive. If they get here before we're done...

"Get them to move it," I yell out the window at the girl.

She repeats the order but with more colourful language.

A thud against the cab from the back and Larry screams, "We're loaded."

The happy sound of the door rolling down fills the cab and Charlie wastes no time shoving the van into drive and hammering the accelerator. We lurch forward and a number of bodies in the back topple over. The corpses are bowled over while our driver smiles as if Death Race 2000 is the main event.

We get to Goodwood Road as the radio comes to life. Mom is chattering, excited. I pick it up and key the mic.

"Slow down." I release the mic and she chatters again. Something that sounds like *I found her*. It makes no sense so I tell her to repeat it.

"I think I found her. Mindy. You said the girl you picked up was too young, right? This one is young, but still looks like she's in her early twenties. Three to four months pregnant from what I can tell and skinnier than that last girl. She must be Mindy, Steve."

I take a breath, not wanting to get my hopes up, but finding anticipation growing inside. "Where?"

"Septic dump on Lake Ridge, just south of Goodwood Road."

Charlie smiles at me.

I key the mic. "On our way."

Mom describes the situation. A mound sits in the centre and it's large. A woman, probably Mindy, is on it. Corpses are all around her but they can't climb the mound, it's too steep. To tease her, it looks like the bikers put a car in the field just outside of the circle. I guess they wanted to taunt her with it. If she tries to get at the car she will be dead quick, if she waits it out she would die of hunger. Thank God the septic dump hasn't been used for a year or we'd be looking at one hell of a mess. It would smell all the same, or would it? One thing about the internet is if you needed information, the thing could get it for you fast.

We come off Lake Ridge and the gate blocks the entrance. Linda, the girl from on top of the container, sits between us. She's a little worse for wear but in good spirits. It seems she didn't stop talking to the people in the container, saying they would all be rescued soon.

"Rush the thing," she yells and braces herself against the dash.

"Go ahead," I agree.

Charlie hits the gas and hammers through the gates. The van bounces. I yell as we hit the lip of the grade and go down. It's a mess of corpses. I spy Mindy right away. For some reason I'm sure it's her. My heart hammers again. We found her.

"You got eyes on her?" Mom says over the radio.

"Got her." I answer. "See our get-away also."

Mindy is on a mound of crap; she needs to come home. About twenty metres away is a car with a sign in the windshield: Keys are on the dash. The corpses are ten metres deep around the mound. They never sleep. Rotted hands reach out and, when one tries to climb the mound it gets less than a metre up before toppling back to land on its stomach. Those that topple crawl up and Mindy meets them halfway with a rock. She's a fighter, but how much longer will she last?

"Charlie, get this thing to attract the corpses. Drop me off at the car, circle around, then use the reverse buzzer to get their attention. I'm going to make sure that car starts before we get her out of there."

He grins at Linda. "Sure thing. You can be shotgun now."

Charlie rolls up to the car and I get out. He drives away fast and a few corpses bounce off the front quarter panel on the way. I get in the car. Keys are on the dash. They go into the ignition smooth as silk, and when I give it a quarter turn, the dash lights up with information. Gas is low but we don't have far to go. Everything looks good.

The beeping of the van backing up attracts the corpses so I give the key another eighth of a turn and pray. Must have done something good in a prior life for the engine catches and comes to life. Sweet.

The radio comes on, but there's nothing being transmitted; all I get is static. It quickly cuts out.

Now I wait. Corpses stumble after the van as it backs up like a pied piper leading rats on their merry way. There's just enough room. Now's my chance.

I put the car into drive and roll it to the foot of the mound Mindy is on. She's already half-way down when I get there and pulls open the door when I stop. Her eyes go wide as she sees me.

"Steve?" She reaches out a hand, touches my face.

I ignore the stench coming off her hand. She must have been up there for a few days. Her hair is a mess and eyes bloodshot. I reach out and take her into my arms, wanting tell her everything is going to be all right now. We made it through another trial. Pa is going to be furious. But instead, all I can do is rely on my superior intelligence.

"Yeah, it's me."

She doesn't seem convinced. There's hesitation in her embrace. A desire to want to verify but not knowing what to do. She pulls away and reaches out again. I take her hand.

"Want to get in? Rescues usually involve you helping out a little, like climbing into the get-away car and such." The beeping of the van is getting closer.

Mindy climbs into the car. I put it into gear and take off, followed by the van.

Charlie has the radio, but that's no concern. Mindy just sits there looking out the passenger window as I steer around another wreck. Inside the trashed mini-van an emaciated hand reaches up and claws at the glass that traps it. Rotting skin leaves a sick smear behind as the hand drops. The spring sun must be cooking the corpse.

I reach out and touch Mindy's hand. She jumps, wide terror fills eyes staring at me before softening. Her hand grasps mine. The corner of her mouth trembles up to smile but fails. Her other hand rubs the bulge of her stomach. I really hope the baby's okay.

We drive north on York Durham Line. The gas light blinks on the dash. I hope there's enough to get us to the lake. If we run out of gas here it's going to be an agonizing two kilometre through woods avoiding booby traps and land mines. Mother is very paranoid.

The greatest thing about our new hideout is the terrain. Steep climbs of dense forest keep out the corpses and the living. It's one of the safest places to be, as long as you don't drink the lake water.

I count the seconds as they pass. The gas light is a steady glare on the dash.

Almost a week. They had her for almost a week. Pa wanted to keep her, even with my child in her belly. He really hates me. Not sure if he's alive now, but at least I have Mindy back. Her straight black hair flutters in the wind. Those small black eyes stare out the window through almond lids. Her hand tightens around mine. Small shoulders start to shrug. Up, down. That beautiful lower lip of hers begins to tremble. A small tear runs down her cheek.

She screams.

It's so abrupt and loud I'm taken off guard. Who would think such small lungs could hold so much? I just let her have at it. Get the madness out. She lets go of my hand and bangs the dash. Her hair falls forward, obscuring those wonderful eyes. I slow, pull over to the shoulder, stop the car.

The air weighs down on us. Time slows. I try to think of something to say but nothing comes. She digs her nails into the dash. The screaming lowers to a whimper. My heart breaks. I want to reach out and hold her. Tell her everything will be all right. But we need to get away from here. I wait for the eternity it will take for her to open up.

It doesn't come.

After ten minutes I put the car into drive and head home.

The intersection of York Durham Line and Tenth Line comes up fast. I touch the brakes but nothing happens. I slam hard on them but the peddle goes to the floor like a dropped fish to the land. I sit there, not moving, as if it took its final breath and no longer cared about the air. The car accelerates.

"You in that car, Steve?" It's Pa's voice. Not sure where it's coming from but it seems like all around.

"Yeah," I say out of reflex.

"Well, if not, then it's your girl and you noticed you have no brakes." There's laughter. "Shut up! Well, I figured it would take a few minutes for you to pump all the brake fluid out of the thing and recorded this for you. The static is a nice touch, don't you think?" He laughs. "Well, now you have no breaks and I tied the linkage into the throttle. No need to try and lift the break peddle, it's jammed now. You'll keep accelerating until you hit something or you run out of gas. Knowing the route you probably took, hitting something sounds like it will happen sooner than later."

I turn to Mindy and mouth the word *fuck*.

"And if you get any ideas of jumping out, just try it. That little chick of yours is not going to have a healthy baby if you hit the pavement rolling at sixty or faster." The flick of a lighter sounds. "Goodbye, Steve. You've been a worthy opponent, until now, that is."

The CD ejects out of the player. I can't believe it. He planned this whole thing. I glare out the window and see the sharp turn signs. The speedometer edges toward eighty.

6

WHAT BRAKES?

The intersection of forty-seven and tenth comes up fast. I pop the car into neutral. The engine revs right up but the incline slows us just enough that I can take the turns. I cut them and drop the car into second, hoping to slow it down somehow. The transmission clunks but we start accelerating again. We're back to eighty in no time and I drop the car back to neutral for the next turn. This one is tight, so I use the shoulder to add friction and bring the speed down again.

My knuckles are white on the wheel.

I take the turn, tires scream, and I try to throw the car into reverse. We need to get away from the dangerous parts and onto Bloomington facing east. If we can slow to a stop, the hike to Mom's is not that bad, even with Mindy in the state she's in.

The engine winds up again so I drop it into low gear once more and then back to neutral. Just need to get into the merge and slow enough to get out. I glance at Mindy. Her eyes are wide and she grips the door white-knuckled.

I wrestle with the wheel. "Just hold on. When we get through the merge get ready to jump out."

"You're kidding, right?" She tightens her grip.

"No, we should be able to slow down enough and let the car go on its own up the road. It'll crash, but without us in it. It sounds bad, but we'll get through it." At least that's what I hope.

She nods, waiting for me to work some magic. I drop the car into gear and play with the hand break until we round the merge. I pull the break up, making the rear drums grind as the engine cries out. The transmission drops into first gear. I wrench the hand break up a little more. We're almost down to twenty. Sweat breaks out on my forehead. Fifteen. Ten.

"Now!"

Mindy Opens the door and is out the car. I drop the break and pop my door open. Pavement rushes at me as I tumble out. The car races, keeps going for a while, then off the road it goes. It ends up in the gully, tires spinning out of control and tearing up grass. Fire from road rash tells me how stupid I am, but instead of examining the injury I look for Mindy. She's a couple of metres away from me and appears to be in one piece.

My back screams at me as I stand. "You okay?" I call out.

"Yes, but I'd rather not do that again."

The car revs like the governor is broke and I wait for the engine to blow. It keeps going, faster and faster. I take a painful step forward and the vehicle is engulfed in a fireball. The concussion throws me back on my ass. Sulphur burns the inside of my nose. He must have rigged it to explode at a certain time. If we'd taken a more direct route to Mom's, we would've been really close when it exploded. Thankfully, the way it's pointed I'd say we were heading to the new estate homes on forty-seven instead of the lake. Eat that, Pa.

I limp over to Mindy. She's not injured, just shaken up. Nothing really rattled her before. Thinking about it, she's been through a lot, but never kidnapped from what I know. We now have something else in common.

"Where's the big cube van?" She takes my hand.

"Probably at the lake by now." I help Mindy to her feed. Blood trickles down my leg and she points to the stain on my pants. I need to wrap something on it or getting back to the lake will be the least of my problems. "We have a lot of walking to do. Feel up to it?"

This centres her thoughts. "Do I have a choice?"

"Not really. Time for you to meet Mom."

Walking any distance with a pregnant Mindy is bad enough, throw in the hills we have to climb and its downright agony. On the way to Mom's, she explains about the biker's raid and how they were taken by surprise. A lot of bikers rode ATVs to get through the woods. It seems they figured out we'd hide some place that had hills to keep the corpses away.

The one good thing about a rural area is less population, but walkers are coming up the hill from behind us. We have to rest and they don't. Another thing to contend with on our way to Mom's place.

Once we turn onto Hillside Dr. and walk into the fields, Mindy seems to understand there's a method to my madness. She sees the large house that marks the end of one of the roads but we just pass by it and into the woods again. We bypass the mines Mom buried in the area and I point out some trip wires. I glance around to make sure the corpses have lost sight of us. If I can't see them, they can't see me.

There's a ridge at this side of the lake but it's not enough to stop us, corpses wouldn't be able to make it up the incline even if they see us. Mindy and I basically support each other as we come out at the clearing and walk the rest of the way, a little slower than before. Okay, I'm supporting her and limping all the way. I bet she's tired if the laboured breathing is any sign. We're covered in sweat and dirt, her more than me because of where she was, but I'm not complaining. I would have done anything to get her back.

The house is there, about forty metres away. Zoey is playing in the back with Colette and she lets out a scream when she sees us.

The big cube van is in the parking lot, and instead of going right to the house, I keep walking. Mindy is a trouper and stays with me.

I want to know who we saved. They must have just gotten there, for the back is open and people are gathering around. Hope it was worth it.

I see Doc climbing out and breathe a sigh of relief. We have our medicine man but he looks as ragged and hungry as the others do. Jill is there, and she's helping Carl out of the van. Shit, looks like the gang's all here for once. I scan the faces for Colette's husband but don't see him. If he's still alive, he may be at one of the other pits holed up like they were. Mom breaks off from the group and walks toward me. Her outstretched arms takes me into a hug.

"Glad you made it." She gives Mindy a good once over, eyes narrowed, but they open up and I know she's going to love this girl regardless. "You must be Mindy."

My gal knows how to butter toast. She holds out her arms for a hug and Mom lets her get squeezed. Guess it has to do with maternal instincts or something.

"Yeah, too bad the old lug here doesn't know how to introduce people."

I wince and take the clue. "Mindy, this is my Mom. Paulette Patterson. Mom, this is Ming, or Mindy."

"Ming Lee, but everyone just calls me Mindy. Glad to meet you."

"You're very pretty," Mom says as she brushes hair out of Mindy's eyes. "Okay, we have a Doc who can check you out now, then I want you to rest up."

"We know him," Mindy says. "He took care of Steve a few times, you know how accident prone he is. And he's been taking care of me since the start of the pregnancy." She motions toward her belly.

"Well, if he knows you, then good, he'll know if anything is wrong." Mom turns back to the group. "Did we get everyone out of hell?"

Colette stares at the group and starts to cry.

———

I rap lightly on the bedroom door before entering. Carl lies in bed and Jill is watching him. She's not letting him do anything but rest and let the gunshot wound in his back heal. I can understand that. Doc checked him out before begging for some food and a place to lie down. I smile and get one from Jill in return. There's nothing to do here, so I go back downstairs.

Colette is a basket case. She's whimpering and nothing Mindy does is helping. She thought her husband would be in the group we picked up. I was hoping for that as well. Having the people we do means a lot. Cindy is even here now along with Danny. The one who started it all off with security meetings last year is now talking with my Mom about what to do. That can't be good.

"Pa and the gang talked to us for a while and then loaded us up in the container." Cindy sips a cup of coffee. "They really are a piece of work over there. The town is all buttoned down with patrols and everything."

"Are they any good?" Mom asks.

"Like I said, they patrol, but it looks like they'd rather be drinking or smoking dope from what I see." She puts the cup down. "Most of them have joints lit when walking around or riding. Don't know where they're getting all the gas from but they're burning a lot of it."

"Most of it would be going bad by now," I say. "Even the stuff in the holding tanks. Water will be collecting in them and it'll start to foul up their machines."

"They have old hogs," Danny says. "Machines like that can take the punishment from bad gas for a long time, just like my Betsy." She motions outside to her plane.

Mindy comes into the living room with a coffee. Caffeine girl needs her fix. Must have driven her mad not getting coffee every morning.

"I want Pa dead," she says not looking at anyone. "He's a son of a bitch and needs to be off this Earth one way or another." She sips the coffee and sighs. "There's a few who will take his place as their new Pa, but they'd be bickering for months to decide which one. They hold elections and all."

"Do we know where this Pa holds up?" Mom asks.

"Some apartment building near the train tracks. I heard them talking that they keep the girls in the apartment near Pa. He likes the place because of the train."

I try to call up the street names in my mind but they don't come. "We need a map. If it's the place I'm thinking of the tracks are right behind the it, near the old Heritage Railway building."

"Yeah, I think that's the one. He can walk out the back and get his locomotive on or head next door to the ladies according to what I overheard." Mindy takes another sip. Her eyes almost roll in ecstasy. "God, I missed coffee."

Mom gives Mindy a sideways look. "You only get one a day while you're carrying my grandson. And besides, we're almost out of the stuff."

"Quick trip into Wallymart will fix that." Mindy grins. "Still lots of stuff in town, right?" She looks back at Mom.

"Not anymore," Mom says. "We cleared the last of it out a week ago. It seems someone else's been in there picking goodies off the shelves as well."

"Okay, I can put up with a lot of shit. Being groped by Pa, getting kidnapped, having to spend three days on a shit pile. You don't dare take away my coffee. We are Canadian, not animals."

"Pa groped you?" I'm in shock. Why would anyone grope a pregnant woman besides her husband? He's a freak and I agree with Mindy; he has to be ended.

"Yeah. They kinda wanted to take turns on me. The only thing I could think of was *let go*. Shitting your pants when they start to mess with their flies stopped them dead."

I can't think. She put up with a lot over the time they had her. Something tells me I'll not hear all of it.

"We need a plan, and a good reconnaissance of the area." Mom levels her gaze at Danny. "You ready to take that plane over enemy territory?"

"Betsy doesn't like getting shot at. And to be out of their range means being too far to see anything well enough to figure it out. Betsy doesn't fly very fast."

"Then let's get one that does." Mom stands. "We're going plane shopping."

I took flying lessons when I was young, even flew a glider. But power planes are a different animal all together. They don't have the lift gliders have, nor are they as responsive. The lessons ended when I couldn't afford to pay anymore. But no one else knew the first thing about planes except Mindy, and Mom played the grandmother card when she said she couldn't fly. If Mom didn't do it, I would have.

Danny agreed to do a run to the airport but wasn't sure where it was. I did. And to make things worse, she wanted something fast in order to spook the bikers into not firing at us. Yes, she "volintold" me to go be her co-pilot. Her logic, if anything happens to her, it would be good to have someone with a little knowledge of what to do. It seems Danny flew for the RAF before she came to Canada. Strange the things you find out about people when there is a need.

When the morning breaks the sky, I'm still staring at the ceiling in my old room. Mindy snores beside me. Not a heavy wood-cutting snore, but a light one, kind of like a chipmunk in heat. She's all cleaned up and Doc saw her before bed. Besides being told to eat a little more, she's as healthy as the others we rescued, but that's not saying much.

Danny wants to get going at first light – now is the time. I climb out of bed, being careful not to wake the pregnant lady, and throw on a housecoat. It's a little cold but not unbearable. I take a quick cold shower in the hall bathroom and hurry downstairs for coffee. Mom is already up and in the kitchen with a cup set aside for me. It's a wonder how well we know each other even after several years apart.

"Danny is outside looking over Betsy," she says. "Did Mindy sleep okay?"

"She's still out." I take a sip of the black gold. "I usually wake her with one of these, but she's been through a lot and I want her to sleep."

"You better wake her before take-off." Mom puts two pans into the oven. "Bread will be ready in about twenty. You can eat and be in the air after."

"Mom, I didn't know what you went through–"

"Enough of that. It's in the past, and we have a future to build for you and that kid of yours." She sits at the table. I join her. "Besides, we went from a small group here to having two pregnant women. That's a good start if you ask me."

I nod, thinking this is a good week for her, minus losing Jeb. First she gets her son back and now the possibility of a grandchild. I take a sip. "I'll need clothes. Didn't really bring much and the ones I left are a little tight."

"You did put on some weight last I saw you. We can get someone to check the homes around here for clothes if you don't mind hand-me-downs."

"No problem with that." The bread is starting to bake, filling the kitchen with amazing smells of childhood. "I did miss this."

"Don't tell me you stopped making your own bread."

"Worked long hours to afford the house. It was easier to just buy it and work than make it."

"By the time you went to the store, picked up the bread, drove home, you could make the stuff and you know what's in it." She shakes her head. "Young people have no idea."

"Well, I do remember how to make it, but where are you getting the yeast?"

"From the plants." She motions outside. "The apples grow and yeast forms on them naturally. You just have to harvest it right and keep the yeast aside. As long as you feed it, the stuff will keep growing."

Still too many things to learn. I'll have to make sure we keep knowledge for the future. That is, if there is one.

Danny comes into the house. She's blowing into her hands. "You're a little late getting up."

"Had to shower and get a coffee," I return.

"Good, that means there's hot water for tea." Danny goes to the stove and grabs the kettle. "Do you have a tea pot?"

"Yes, as long as you don't mind herbal tea."

"Not a problem."

I wait while they make a pot of tea. When it's put aside to steep, I pop the question. "What type of plane do you want?"

"A single prop Cessna will do but if they have a jet, I'll take that. We can then pass over them fast and they won't have time to shoot at us."

"What about fuel?"

"Nav fuel for jets is a lot different than that for piston pounders. It's more like kerosene than anything else. Lasts a lot longer than you think." She glances over at the tea. "Damn for steeping. I used to have a pot that turned on for me before I woke up. Fresh brewed tea in the morning is the best."

"Won't the planes be rusted out?"

"Depends if they have them in hangers or stored outside. If done correctly, even outside storage is okay for a jet. Less moving parts in the engine, or is that more? Never could remember that."

Mom stands up and opens the oven. "You should have a ground crew."

"The fewer people we have to worry about the better." Danny checks the tea pot. "If we need to get in and out fast, it's best to just have just two people and Betsy. We won't have to worry about anyone else being around for the problems. Besides, is anyone trained as ground crew in here?"

We both shake our heads.

"Then it's settled, just Steve and me will go. You all just wait here and don't worry about anything."

Mom turns the bread around in the oven, straitens up, and walks to the cupboard. "Then you'll need this." She pulls out a case. "The battery is charged and it will hold a lot of pictures. The thing cost enough so it's about time we used it for something other than taking pictures of birds and cats."

"You don't have a cat," I say.

"No, but one's been snooping around the place the last couple of days and I think she's more tame than wild."

She holds the camera out for me. It's a simple SLR digital with a telephoto zoom. Worth a lot of money before the world broke. I turn it on and tab through the pictures. Birds flying, birds in trees, birds on the ground, bird in a cat's mouth. Interesting, the cat is a tabby. Samantha!

"When's the last time you saw the cat?" I ask.

"Just this morning before you came down. She's in the woods most of the day hunting. Why?"

"I think you found my cat."

7

EYE IN THE SKY

I want my life to be as normal as possible. Part of that is achieved already with Mindy being rescued. Part is not, like having my home back, a community, and maybe a job again. But another part, one I never thought would be there, was Samantha. My cat is five years old. A tank when you look at her, but so sweet it's unbelievable. And I thought I had lost her. Now, there's pictures. I'm positive it's her. The markings, goofy look, the way she prances on the grass as if it's beneath her to be outside. Everything. And I want my little ball of fur by my side again. Besides, she's a great mouser and Mom's home needs that, even if she won't admit it.

Danny taps me on the shoulder. "We have a plane to catch."

"Hell." I turn the camera off to look at Mom. "Okay, but when we get back, I want you to take me to exactly where you got these pictures."

"Sure, but what do you want with the cat?"

"She's mine," I say. "Anyway, Mindy needs Sam just as much as Sam needs her." I sling the camera over my shoulder. "I know you've never been one for animals, but there's a certain something about a cat you have to admire."

"And besides pooping in the house, what is that?"

"They're good at catching prey." I longingly stare at the oven where the bread is finishing off, and turn to Danny. "Time to fly."

"I suggest you get dressed first," she says with a laugh.

I look down, the bathrobe is almost open to reveal me in all my glory.

Mom's washed my clothes and they are almost dry. I pick the pants that are the least damp along with a t-shirt. Socks are another story, all of them are still wet. Don't want to catch a cold.

I make my way downstairs after kissing Mindy. Danny is already outside fussing over the plane. Mom is there at the door holding two things for me, a sweater and socks. She presents them with a smile.

"I could never throw out your father's things," she says, watching me put on the socks. "To toss them was to admit he was completely gone." Tears well in her eyes.

The sweater is one of those zipper neck ones. Cords of wool with a high neck will keep me warm in the biplane and happy in whatever we find from there. It smells of moth balls, but I welcome it. Nothing says grown up like wearing your Dad's hand-me downs.

"You look very much like him," Mom says. "Good strong chin and drooping eyebrows." She hugs me. "Be careful out there. I know Danny's been with us only a few days, so make sure you come home in one piece. And don't forget to get good pictures of what they're doing out there." She opens the hallway closet and pulls out a leather jacket. "Your father wanted you to have this when you got older. Never did get a chance to give it to you, but I guess now's as good as ever."

I stare at the jacket, taking in the badge sown on the shoulder, RCR 3rd Battalion. Dad served? The whole thought of wearing something of Dad's suddenly makes my head light. A certain pride wells up inside me as I slip on the jacket that means so much. I want to show how much it means to me, knowing Mom dug up a painful reminder of her long dead husband and gave me what amounts to pride in remembering what he once was, an elite fighting force, the Royal Canadian Regiment.

"Your father wore that while training at the Mountain Warfare Training Centre in California. The General there found out you don't park your jeep in the way of the RCR when they're on a run. Instead of breaking ranks, the men just climbed over the jeep and kept running. The General couldn't believe they stayed in perfect formation while doing it and no one ever parked in their path again. Your father commanded them until he was shot."

Dad was shot? Why didn't I know this? "When did that happen?"

"Before we met, well before you. That's why he wasn't in the military when you were born." She pulls out a case from the top shelf of the closet. "You never saw this, though I was proud he had it, he wasn't. Said if he deserved it all the men would have survived. Instead, he could only pull out two of the four men wounded in a fire fight."

She opens the case and I stare at a gold medal. Four wide points with maple leafs between them decorate the outside circle of silver leaf. In the middle, a gold maple leaf sits on a red enamel background. A red ribbon with two vertical white strips, the ribbon for fastening it to a uniform. The Star of Military Valour. Dad was a hero. With a respectful glance at Mom, I reach out and touch the raised surfaces to etch it into my mind. I remember reading something about there only being a very limited amount of these given out, and the first one only after thirteen years after they created it. But if Dad left the forces before I was born, that would mean... my brow furrows.

"Yes, he was awarded this after being medically discharged," Mom says. "He looked good in his parade dress. You were just a glimmer in our eyes at that time. I want you to remember him the way he was, before and after you were born."

"I will." I take a deep breath. "I'll remember it, promise. And you'll tell it to your grandchild in a couple of months." The smile on her face tells me she will, and more. "We'll never forget Dad, or any of the others who saved the lives of people in our camp. But now, I gotta catch a plane."

Danny takes a roundabout way to get us to the airport. She flies north for ten minutes, loops west, then heads south. We're far enough from the airport that we cannot really see it but I point to where it should be, due east. She drops one wing and pulls back on the stick. I'm pushed into my seat.

"Having fun back there?" she yells over her shoulder.

"Oh, lots," I say. "Rather be flying myself. Loved gliders."

She laughs, straightens out the plane, and dives to tree top level. "This way they won't get a bead on us until we're about to land."

I don't understand what she's doing; there's hardly any trees besides a few lines of them. Most of the area is farm land. She takes us down even closer to the ground, like three metres.

"I crop dusted for a living. This is fun!"

We're going fast for a biplane. Probably over a hundred. She can land it going forty, and take-off at the same speed. We pass McCowan Road and the Markham Fairgrounds.

Danny points down. "What's down there?"

"Last I remember they had a shoe sale going on," I say. "We could stop there if you want on the way back. Surprise people with what we find."

"Sounds good. A lot of people seem to need shoes."

I see a few corpses wandering around but not enough to really worry about. To the south, a wall of corpses staggers out of the top end of Markham. They must be on the move again.

I point south. "We have to hit it before those get there."

"If we buzz them heading west they'll start to walk that way." A buzzer starts to cry for attention. "Damn, afraid of that."

"What?"

"We've got a leak in the tank somewhere. Do you smell gas?"

Sounds like a reasonable thing to ask. The prop is in front of the plane and we have no canopy. Going about a hundred the fumes could be noticed. Yeah, right. "You're kidding, right?"

"Just put your head down by your knees and tell me if you smell anything."

I do what I'm told and bend over. The section is cramped but not too much. I take a whiff. For some reason it works, gas fumes hit me. A quick push off and I'm sitting up straight again. "We got gas."

"The bottling type of gas or the crap we're leaking kind?" Danny's not looking back now. The airport is coming up and she points at it to verify.

"The *oh my God we're going to drop out of the sky* type!"

She pulls back on the throttle as we come up to Highway forty-eight. "Well, we'll have to patch it before going home. Need to fill up with juice as well. Hope this place has a secured tanker or something."

We first fly over the plane parking area to scout what's there. I realize the jets all have their wings removed except two, but they appear to be old and rusted.

"Holley shit!" Danny points. "Do you see that baby down there?"

I crane my neck to see what she's pointing at. "Where?"

"Right there, just below us. Oh, I've always wanted to fly one of those." She pushes the throttle back up and banks south a little. "Hold on, we're going in."

Danny turns us back to the north hard, throwing my stomach near to my knees, and holds it until we're just about lined up for the runway. We're not out that far, only to Ninth Line, so she has to work in order to get things lined up and the plane at the right altitude which causes my stomach to jump. She touches down with ease and we come rolling to a stop near some containers. The grass has grown so much I'm worried we'd be cutting in when we lurch forward with a little more power. We lumber over the rough shoulder as she drives the plane off the runway and toward some cargo containers.

I unbuckle and sit up on the fuselage, waiting for her to bring us to a stop. When she does, we're near the fuel tanks and a small jet plane.

"We're so lucky!" she cries out. "My God, a Viperjet, MK III. And she looks brand new."

I study the plane. Its sleek wings barely sweep back. There are two intakes below the cabin, one on either side. It screams power and speed except for all the dust and dirt on it.

Years ago I watched an old James Bond movie where 007 jumped into a small jet and flew around for a while. This is bigger, but it reeks of speed. Danny is all but hugging the thing. Her hand wipes away dust covering the cockpit and she stares into it.

"Check the tank and see if they have anything in her. If so, we'll need to drain it and feed this baby some real fresh stuff. It should have three tanks so check them all."

The fuel tanks are full. All three of them. Av fuel is to the top of the tanks so much that I can put a finger in and get it wet. "All full to the brim. What's so special about this thing?"

"Besides being fast, it's manoeuvrable and small. No one's going to be able to hit this baby when we fly by." She pops the canopy. "Oh, she even has keys."

I glance inside. Keys are sitting on the seat. The rich haven't a care in the world. That is, until last year when money became nothing to the corpses. "What do we need?"

"First, patch up Betsy and get her filled up. Second, this thing eats gas like no tomorrow. I want the tanks drained and refilled, then get her on the runway before I fire her up. That's a big difference with this thing for we can bingo fuel in one tank with take-off alone. Third, we'll do a checklist to make sure she's safe and cleaned up a little. I don't want to worry about keeping her air born while watching where we're going. And fourth, we'll take off and be in Uxbridge within five minutes."

I blink. "Five minutes?"

"Within five minutes, probably less. Yes, this thing can go like a bat out of hell."

Danny sits in the pilot's seat and I'm behind her in the passenger's. If I was claustrophobic, the plane would have me crawling on edge. I've been in sport cars with more room. My arms are resting on the side of the plane with my fingers staying clear of all the buttons. There's a stick between my legs, but Danny's told me not to touch it. She hasn't fired it up, but I'm waiting for the blast. We found two helmets under the back seat while looking for fuses, and we're plugged in and ready. Harnesses are tight. I wait for the show.

The pilot's seat has more buttons and switches than I've seen in my life. The display is two screens the size of iPads and they both boast buttons up and down each side as well as underneath. I have no idea what the hell they're for. On the left is the throttle and canopy lock.

She puts in the key and gives it a little turn.

I expect the engine to come to life just like a car, but it doesn't. The instruments light up and displays start their checks. Soon, all the lights are green and Danny hits a button to bring up one of the displays. It's a map overlay. Damn thing has built in navigation. Talk about being sweet.

Danny glances over her should and shouts, "You ready?"

The mic on the helmet picks it up and my ears explode with her voice. "We have mics now, remember?" I say.

"Sorry," she says in a more controlled voice. "Forgot with all this excitement."

"You'll have to show me how to operate this thing once we're done."

"Any time."

She reaches forward and flips a few switches. A pump starts and air comes from one of my armrests. She lifts the red covered switch on the right.

"Ignition." A flip and the turbines start to turn, picking up speed until air rushes into them. The engine sparks to life and a high-power whine reverberates before it disappears behind a howl of power.

"Man, this is better than sex!" Danny squeals.

"I'll remember that when you get horny or something." I glance around, half expecting corpses to start coming out now the noise is a factor, but then again, we landed and none came out. "We about ready to take-off?"

She pulls the red lever and the canopy comes down to an almost close. "Yes, we're just about ready."

Danny hasn't given us gas but the plane, even in idle, creeps forward. She pulls back on the canopy lock and giggles a little.

"You need a cold shower?" I ask.

Danny laughs. "Look at the fuel gauge." She taps it. "We're already down four litres on the first tank and that's just starting this beast."

"Then we better take off, unless you want to idle us bone dry."

"Roger that."

She pushes the throttle forward. I don't know what I was expecting. G-force shoves me into the seat as the plane hauls ass down the runway. At about a third of the way down we're going seventy. At the half-way point, our ground speed is over ninety and Danny pulls back on the stick. The pull of the earth yanks me down into the seat as the wheels lift from the ground. Danny hits the gear switch. A winding pierces my ears as the landing gear pulls up into the nose and wings of the small plane. We're hitting three G's when Danny eases back on the throttle, levelling us off. I glance at the altimeter on the back of her seat. We're at 1,500 metres and going 710 k/ph. Damn, a lot faster than a prop plane or glider.

We pass Goodwood in under a minute and come up to Uxbridge. Danny noses down and we pick up speed. She's insane.

"Warning, ground. Warning, Ground." A metallic voice drowns in our ears when we get to thirty metres. The voice keeps going until Danny hits an override. We're blasting at 910 k/ph and the ground is close enough for me to count each blade of grass between the railroad ties. She's following the tracks. Fast and low, that's what she said we'd have to do, and she's keeping her promise.

I have the camera out and start tracking the buildings, taking pictures like I have nothing better to do in life. Must get as much as possible. Biker pissing on a tree, check. Biker scared shitless on his bike, check. Supposedly Pa's building, check. His girl house, check. I don't lift my finger from the shutter until all I see is trees. Good thing this is one of those top of the line cameras.

"Get everything?" Danny asks.

"Think so. About twenty pictures or so. We're going fast, you know."

She pulls back on the stick and I'm pressed into my seat, feeling as if I'm weighing in at over three hundred kilo's. "Change it to movie and we'll fly the tracks again."

Movie, why didn't I think of that.

We hit over 3,000 metres and Danny slows the bird down and punches the rudder to the right. The left wing makes a lazy pull over the plane and then we're diving again. She has the throttle all the way open to get fast right away. The little voice inside my head starts the mantra early due to our velocity.

When Danny pulls back to level out I'm truly concerned we're going to hit the ground, but instead we're just a few metres from that. Going to have to change my pants when we get home. I have the camera pointed to the left and run the record for all I'm worth.

Pa is outside his house, and as we go by I give him the royal salute. He probably doesn't see it. A couple of the bikers aim guns and rifles at us but Danny doesn't do anything to evade. We just fly past and climb when we're out of town.

"Where to now?" Danny asks.

"How much fuel we have?"

"Probably about an hour before we need to switch to the last tank. Depending on how we use it."

I smile a little. "How about we buzz Mom's place and then head north east to see what it's like in Newmarket and Bradford?"

"Sounds like a plan. Why there?"

"There's a Costco in north Newmarket and I want to see how it held up. We could also check the one in Richmond Hill and then south Markham. Good way to see what's happening in the cities as well."

"Like the way you think, Steve."

We reach Mon's fast and buzz them at about twenty metres. Not as close as we did Uxbridge but close enough to make everyone scatter who was out early. Newmarket comes up just as fast and I direct Danny on where to find the Costco. It's not trashed. In fact, it looks like no one opened it when the world went to crap. It maybe a good place to raid later on.

Bradford is packed with corpses. They seem to be stuck due to the way the town was built. None of them are heading for the bridge, but a number of them are in the streams fed by Lake Simcoe. No way am I eating fish out of there.

Heading south, the Richmond Hill Costco appears to have been open that horrible day last year. Corpses are milling about. Some try to follow us as we zip by. The Markham warehouse is a mess of burnt buildings. Most of the houses in the area have been razed to the ground in a fire, or so it seems.

Danny does a sweeping bank and points us north. "Let's put this baby to bed," she says.

"Yes, let's do that, and get home with what we have."

8

HELL RIDERS

Mom sits at the table with Danny beside her. Mindy sits beside me. Jill is on the other side and Cindy sits next to Doc on the opposite. It appears our war council is complete with the addition of two others. I miss Carl being here, for it's four votes to two if the guys say anything. And you better believe Mom and Mindy will want to keep me out of harm's way if they can, but I intend to thwart it when they attack anything I volunteer for.

"There's no way we'll let Danny do another fly by with Betsy. As you said, there's a leak in the gas tank." Mom taps her finger on the table to make a point.

"But Steve and I repaired it at the airport." Danny's a flyer and brave as shit. She wants to help out and being our air support is the best thing she could do. "And besides, the other planes there are either closed tops or too small for anything."

"Steve, you're going to have to keep from getting yourself killed," Jill says. Finally, someone who thinks we're on the right track. "That way Carl can kick your ass when he's better."

I straighten. "I didn't do anything to Carl."

Mindy comes to my aid. "Yeah, Steve tried to help him."

"Last time you guys worked on one of your plans, he got shot in

the back. I don't want any more holes in him unless I put them there."
Jill imitates my mother's finger jab at the table.

Doc takes a deep breath and looks straight at me. "Steve, your plan is to go in and kill Pa, right?"

"Yes," I say.

"And you want to use the tracks to do it, right?"

"Again, yes. I outlined this all just a few hours ago." My leg twitches and Mindy lays a hand on my thigh.

"So, how are you going to use the tracks if the train is parked in Uxbridge?"

Fuck, Doc saw the flaw in my plan, or figured out I was going to do something stupid like go on foot. "I'll use one of the bikes," I say, referring to the electric ATVs my mom has. Thank God for her having the place decked out with solar panels. "They're really quiet and fast enough. If the bikers come after me then I'll ditch it and go through the woods."

Doc nods, rubs his chin. "But how are you going to get close enough to him?"

I smile. "I'm not." Everyone starts to ask "how" at once. They all stare at me, even Mindy. But I hold my ground.

"Okay, I'll bite," Jill says. "Tell me, Mr. Macho, how do you intend to kill the bastard if you're not close to him?"

"With a high power rifle and scope," I say, smiling at everyone around me. "Don't need to be close in order to put a bullet through his forehead if you have enough oomph behind the shot."

I know the argument is sound, it's just when and how that bothers me. Do I make it happen during the day or night? If at night, how do I get there without being seen? Same for the day. It's a bitch when things work out wrong, and this little play is going to be something else.

"You're going to ride one of my ATVs on the track for how long?" Mom has that type of stare right now that says she wants to make sure she gets her stuff back.

"Not long." I stand up and take out an area map. It's hard to believe they were still printing them just before the world went to shit, but I guess not everyone had access to the network, especially if they're out of town. Roaming charges in Canada were a bitch. "Right here is where I'll start my trek." I put a finger on the end of Sandy Hook Road. "It's part of the Trans Canada Trial so it should be good." I move my finger along. "Here, at Concession seven, I'll hide the bike in the parking lot of the water pollution control plant and hike the rest of the way to the concrete plant, here." I jab my finger on the spot. It's close to Pa's house but still a good distance away, around eighty metres. "I'll set up and wait there. When I get a good shot, bang! Pa's gone."

Mindy's nodding at this plan. Good, the one person I really need to accept it is her. If she didn't like it and I did it anyway, well, I'd never hear the end of it.

"Okay, say you do this," Jill says. "You'll need backup, like a spotter or something. I remember the movies and all the snipers had a look out. Someone who targeted the person and made sure the coast was clear to fire."

Cindy levels her gaze at Jill. "You volunteering?"

"Well, I could do it," she says. "But I hate being around the lug too much. He smells and farts a lot."

Mindy lets out a snort. "You should sleep with him. He snores as well."

Mom rolls her eyes.

"I know you guys play around a lot, but we need to get this plan nailed down before the bikers start to wonder what the plane was doing this morning. If they get curious, like I know they will, they'll start searching. How long before they decide the blockade on the drive is not just natural fall from the trees after a storm? Or, if the path between the houses are a little too well worn? Then what will we do?" Cindy glares at me.

"And Pa has a real hard-on for you, Steve," Mindy says. "I had to endure that story about the elastics and then he started to talk about what he was going to do to you when he catches you. Don't get caught."

I hear her, but I also know it has to be done and now. Work in the day or night, that's the only question. And I can see a lot of good things about both, so how do I decide which one to do? Flip a mental coin? That's not going to work. I glance around the table and everyone is looking at me, even Mindy. They're waiting for me to make the call on how I want to kill, or how I want to get caught. Either way, not that great. But Pa has to be killed. He's not just our enemy, but a bad person with no moral compass. Who else would torture a complete stranger for a whole week just for the fun of it?

"I'm going in tonight." I fold up the map.

Danny is packing up the plane with some home-made drop bombs Mom made. I've got my weapon and the bike will be ready in another hour while it charges by solar cell. Jill is talking about how we're going to do this, but she doesn't realize I've made up my mind. Bullet to the head. Jill wants me to shoot his balls off first, make him suffer. That's not the way I roll. One bullet, ninety yards, right in the brain. He'll be dead and done before they know what happened. And we'll be running up the tracks to get our bikes and head home in a round-about way.

I thought of not letting Jill come. No need to put her in harm's way, especially since her body is still recovering from being locked up, but she made the argument. If she didn't go then Mindy would demand to, and there's no way I'm putting her in harm's way, especially not while she's carrying my child. And Carl's in bed resting while that bullet hole heals. If I need someone to come with me, Jill is the best choice. Strong, confident, bullet proof. Well, almost bullet proof.

She knows Pa, and hates him just as much as I do. I would still have my house if it wasn't for those bikers. Their greed and way of dealing with people put them on the outs with us all from the start. Heck, maybe what's went on is the best thing to happened to us all; it's brought us together to face one enemy and get rid of them instead of letting the politicians screw everything up. At least there's no debt to worry about for Ontario, or Canada for that matter. We can just go along our merry way and rebuild. This time we better make it illegal to tax people to death. But then again, we'll need to deal with the corpses first.

Jill taps me on the shoulder, breaking me out of the daydream.

"If you fire that canon, everyone will know where we are." She points to the rifle I'm carrying. "Have you got a suppressor for it?"

Shit, she's right. "No, never looked for one."

"Then we stop by Carl's place on the way and pick something up."

I look down. Two feet still attached. Brain, well, that's another story. "You may not know this, but they burnt everything to the ground."

She laughs. "I doubt that. Besides, baby had a lot of surprises buried around the yard."

"What you mean?"

"Just a little in the forest is a shop where he made the suppressors for the gun club. In there he has a few high power rifles and you can kill two birds with one stone, get a better rifle and a suppressor so no one knows where we are when the thing goes off." She glances at the scope. "And maybe a night vision scope would help."

I stare blankly at her.

"You didn't think of these things, did you?" Jill gives me a humourless smile. "That's why you need me around, Steve, to make sure you don't get yourself killed." She walks away, whistling a little tune as she goes.

The skeleton of Carl's home looms over us as we drive onto the property. Such a waste. It reminds me of all the carnage the bikers brought to our town. At least the forest didn't catch fire. It only takes a few minutes to find the shed out back at Carl's place. To call it a shed, though, is an understatement. It's more like a workshop on steroids. Like he did with the house, the shop has solar panels and batteries all working hard. How Jill knows all this I'll just chock up to Carl trusting her. Funny how he never told me about the place. Nice little lathe and work benches, and four safes for rifles and guns. On the wall to the left of the safes are shelves of suppressors. He really loves playing with them.

Jill heads to one safe and runs the combination. When it opens, I whistle. Snuggled into a holder sits a Smith & Wesson M&P 15. No mars on the thing and I can still see a little grease in the receiver. This is what I was looking for. Good muzzle break to hide the flash, takes Nato .556 ammo that's easy to find, and the beast is semi-auto to boot! She pulls the rifle out and hands it to me.

Next we find the suppressor made for the rifle. Carl loves to shoot. He made suppressors in order to keep the complaints down. Jill holds one out that looks almost like an old soda bottle from the '70s and smiles. Must be the best one available.

Jill pulls me to the last safe on the wall. She spins the combo and opens it revealing all the ammo one would need. From .202 all the way up to heavy loads for magnums. I grab the .556 and pick out an extended clip. I'll need this in order to be safe. Never know when you need more than one shot.

As I load the clips, Jill picks out another rifle. I start to salivate. How did I miss the Mossberg? She lays it down on the bench and spreads her arms as a sales person would. "The M&P 15 is good if you're just out shooting some bear or something, but you really need to have something like this little girl." She picks it up and pulls back the bolt. "The Mossberg MVP LC, light-chassis, bolt-action with Vortex, and HS-t scope fitted with dark sight is the one you want. Its light weight, has an adjustable chin rest, bi-pod for sure aim, and an adjustable trigger all the way up to seven pounds." She slams the bolt home. "AR 15 will allow you to reload quick after each shot and has really good accuracy without losing punching power at greater distances." She holds it out to me. "Use the Smith if we need quick shots, but the Mossberg is what you want to kill Pa." A box of rounds hits the table. "And these have hollow points to make sure he's dead."

The early evening air caresses my face as we ride along Wagg Road to Lake Ridge, then up Ganton Road. We take it to O'Neil Road and North to the trail. A quick scoot and we pass the blocking gate that stops people from doing what we are at this point, and gun across the path with our lights shielded. The sun is starting to hit the horizon so we only have a short time to get to where we're going before darkness removes our ability to drive without lights.

At the water plant, we head off the trail well before the road, and park the ATVs just behind the building. My ass hurts from the ride and I stretch to get some feeling back into my legs. The rest is on foot, so it's going to take a lot longer than I want, but at least the light is low, making it harder to see us.

We stay in the shadows as best as we can, sneaking to Main Street and walking to the Pool and Spa shop. I'm hoping if anyone see us it'll look like we're shopping for something to keep us busy at night. Hopefully no one else is thinking the same thing. I pick up the pace, jog around the building and spy the path. We walk down it, trying to keep to the darkness until the concrete plant. A small wire fence offers little if no barrier as I put a foot over it. Off the trail and into their yard. It's easy enough to climb one of the shoots and get to the roof, but upon looking at the area I call that spot no joy. There's a small building just south of the big factory, probably the offices for the plant. I want to use that instead.

Jill gives the knob on the door a little twist. It opens and we enter crouched down. I fumble for a light until Jill drops a small glow stick. Good thing she came along. The stairs lead us to the top level and more offices. One faces Pa's home, so we enter it. Small, but not that bad. The place smells a little and the corpse sitting at the desk is why. There's a note on a stack of papers and the back of its head is blown off. A small revolver dangles in an emaciated hand. He must have understood what was happening and decided it wasn't for him.

The window is open a crack and Jill makes that about thirty centimetres. Just perfect for what we need. I drag the chair and occupant out of the office and then push the desk against the window so I can lay on it. A quick sweep of my arm removes all that's on it, including the small computer. It hits the floor with a thud that makes Jill cringe. I drop the bi-pod legs and go prone on the desk.

Night vision optics are great when you're used to them, I'm not. Everything is in shades of green and a little fuzzy. I play with the sight and then give up when I can't get it any better. It's a good scope – brings the back windows into great focus for me. I look for one with a light on. From what Mindy told us, Pa will be in one of the top floor suites so he can look out at the train. The historical society ran the train until all the volunteers either passed away or got too old to do anything. They never sold the tracks, though. The thought was someone would bring it back for the public and charge them an arm and leg to ride the thing. It was always the bane of the people in the area they drove through. Loud, evasive, and most of the guys who ran it were crusty old men.

The rumble of Harley's in the distance breaks the calm. Must be one of the patrols. On our flight we saw a number of them riding around doing nothing but looking. Guess they are on high-alert after the jet flew over. Nothing scares criminals more than the thought of being caught and punished. Well, maybe another gang taking over their turf would cause them issues.

One bike is really close, or the muffler is so dead it doesn't do anything. I swear it has to be right under the window. A quick gesture and Jill looks out and down. It's really dark now. No light except that dying glow in the west. It helps a little, but not much. Should be a partial moon tonight; that will light our way.

The rumbling increases in volume and lights play on the street out near Pa's place. I point the rifle down a little but cannot see past the old rail cars. The bikes backfire and silence comes to the air. More lights brighten the area but these aren't headlights, but regular flashlights. The top floor brightens on the women's building.

Screams rupture the silence and laughter floats in the air. I cannot image what they're doing, but remember they went after young women and teens. I swipe the rifle to the left a little and get an eyeful of long red hair on top of a young head as she tries to fight off the old, ugly biker feeling her breasts. Bile rises in my throat. One simple shot and that girl will be free, but we'll never get another chance to take out Pa again. Not like this.

Fuck. I hate decisions. The lesser of two evils. The old ugly biker probably is low on the food chain. I sweep right and angle back on Pa's place. Lights dance in the rooms a little. Someone must be making things a little more comfortable. A chill breeze comes through the window and I shiver even in the sweater Mom gave me. I concentrate on my breathing. In, hold, out. In, hold, out. The best way to hit a target is to squeeze the trigger between your heart beats. Time the squeeze for when you hold. Make every shot count. You can do this.

A bearded face appears at Pa's window. I'm sighted in. Jill is muttering "Fire".

In. Beat. Hold. Beat. Squeeze. Fire.

9

RUN AWAY

The rifle bucks back into my shoulder. The high velocity-round travels the distance in less than a heartbeat and shatters glass. Blood spatters the wall in the room. Big, red, and ugly. The prettiest sight I've seen in a long time. Head shot. No returning. Not even as a corpse. Pa's gone. We don't have time to wait around to deliberate, time to go.

Bikes fire up outside. Loud thumping engines try to burn gas with too much water in them. Wonder if they figured out the direction of the shot. Maybe, maybe not. There's nothing left to do but exit and get home. Run away. Like that bad Monty Python movie Mom made me watch long ago. Only this time, I'm the bunny with the big teeth.

I don't feel bad about killing the man. Actually, there's more relief than anything else. Pa's tried to kill me several times, inflicted injury and mayhem on my world, and nothing I really did should have merited such treatment. Hell, the first time we met the bikers, all we were doing was getting supplies. It's not like they built the Wallymart we raided. But they did want to take the women. Jill and Mindy, the two I had with me. It's not that I owned them. Hell, I don't think anyone could own either of those head strong ladies. Not now. Jill's became stronger than ever. Her whole life outlook changed when she met Carl, and from there her strength just grew. Mindy, God bless her, is the woman I love. Nothing will stop her from trying to get back to me. Nothing. And if anything does happen, I've helped educate her in survival, so much that she will survive. Heck, Mom will make sure of it. And I would hate to be the one who crosses my mother.

"Let's move," I say.

We stand and follow the glow sticks out the building. Instead of hitting the railroad tracks right away, we've planned to race to the north factory and cross over Main Street at that point. Then we'll get our ATVs from behind the water plant and retrace our steps from there. Should be easy enough, but then again, nothing is easy when it comes to a planned escape.

More Hogs fire up. Screams pierce the night air. Someone found the body. The edges of my mouth lift. They'll be in turmoil for a while with infighting to pick a new leader. Hopefully, this will give us time. That is until a new leader can take Pa's place and regroup them all.

Headlights flash in the concrete manufacturer's parking lot as we duck into the bushes to the east. They figured out where we shot from. That's no real surprise. It's the only building facing into the area with a good enough vantage point.

Once the group settles down to examine the building, we take off through the back of the lot. A fence sections off only part of the lot and we get to the walking path easily. We hide in the shadow as bike after bike drives north on Main Street. I really want to start taking them down with the AR 15 but Jill makes we wait. Probably a good idea. If we announced our presence the group will converge and we'll be dead in no time.

There's a break in the bikes. Not much of one, but I hear it. We sprint across the road, a distant headlight outlines us for those already past. If anyone is looking in their mirror, they'll know we're here. I don't breathe while we run. Just pump arms and legs to get across as fast as possible.

An engine guns.

A shot rings out.

We're across the street.

Still, there's only open ground until we can get beside the plant and into darkness. Five heartbeats. Ten. Twenty. I breathe once more, taking in lung full after lung full of air. Sweat pours down my body. Too much too fast. My heart is on the verge of bursting.

We reach the building's edge and I slump down only to have Jill pull me back up. We keep running. Thirty metres and we hit the other corner. The place we left the ATVs. I don't look, just hop on mine hoping Jill is hopping on hers.

One quick flip turns the power on and I kill the headlight, not wanting to reveal our spot. A gun cocks in my ear.

"Now, ya don't wanna leave without saying goodbye, do you, Steve?"

I recognize the voice. "Pa?"

"Why'd ya go and shoot up my brother's room?" He steps out of the shadows and into view. The left side of his body and face are covered in sticky blood. The elastics hold his beard in a tight braid. "What did Peter do to you?"

My head spins. I shot the wrong man. Frustration boils in me. I grip the handles of the ATV and jerk upward four times. "What do I have to do to kill you?"

"Probably more than I'm going to do to kill you." He smiles, yellow and uneven teeth almost glow in the moonlight. The glint of a hand cannon pointed at my head is a warning. "I think I'll make an example out of you. Rescuing all those people without getting a single person bit was entertaining. Who's the sky jockey?"

"No one you know." I scramble through scenarios on how to get past this encounter. Mindy needs me. Hell, my unborn child needs me. But this is the end. Nothing I can do will fix what's about to happen. Pa is the devil and he's done it. No way he will play the put-me-on-the-mound game again. Not even torture for any length of time, unless he knows I'll not be able to run away or fight back. Despair chases away the frustration.

"Turn off the bike, Steve. We need to talk."

He uses the gun to motion me down. I comply, dismounting on the left. "What are we talking about?"

He backs me up against a wall. His feted breath claws at me. I don't want to look in those eyes again. Something about them pulls the strings of every nerve I have, but how to not stare when a gun is at your head? Nothing I can do now but listen to what he has to say.

"The jet was a nice touch. Where'd you get it?"

"It's a kit. Found it at one of the rich homes."

He strikes me with the butt, right on the forehead. Pain races through my skull. "Try again. We checked out all the rich homes last month. Nothing like that was in any of them."

"You missed one," I lie. "Just think. There's more in the forests than you realize."

"Humph, probably." He uses the barrel of the gun to scratch his face. "But really unlikely. The gang's been conditioned to put everything it finds into a kitty." He narrows his eyes at me and lets out a soft laugh. "Oh, aren't you the smart one. Getting me talking while the owner of the other bike finds a way around us to sneak up." He grabs me by the throat. My breath is cut off. With a jerk he pulls me close. Eyes laced with red lines stare into mine for a second as a sneer crosses his face. He flips me around so my back is against him. "Okay, who's out there? Show yourself or Steve gets it."

Nothing. He spins us around, faces the way I came. "Come on. I don't have all day to wait for you!"

I pray Jill's smart enough to just leave.

Pa spins me around to face him again. "Call 'em out."

"No," I answer flatly. A denial Pa probably doesn't hear very often.

His eyes narrow. Brow furrows. The creaking of his palm clasping the gun's grip becomes audible. "Yes, or I'll–"

I need to give Jill more time. "You'll what? Torture me? Put a bullet into my head?"

"Something like that. Probably torture ya, kill ya, and dump ya close to the new place ya have. Let your loved ones put a bullet into your head." He smiles, one corner of his mouth reaching higher than the other.

Sweat beads on my forehead. My heart pounds to get blood past his iron grip. I steal a glance to the right, hoping to see a shadow running away. Anything to show my sacrifice has saved a friend. But I don't want to die. Not now. Too many relying on me to live.

"Then go ahead and get it over with, will you." I spit into his face, trying to infuriate him into killing me on the spot. Mom would be angry with me for doing it; her thoughts would be to survive until you find a way out and then run like a thief in the night, cutting as many throats as you can. But I'm not that type of person. I want to say planning is my forte, and now this creep has taken that away from me. All that's left for me is to get killed and hope he does it in such a way that I don't come back.

He jams the muzzle of the gun into my mouth. My teeth scream out. Pa's eyes are wide. "Is this what you want?"

I nod. A muffled "do it" makes its way out of my mouth. The cold metal zaps off one of my oldest fillings. A tear lazily rolls out of the corner of my eye. If I anger him enough…

"I could do it, you know. Pull the trigger." His voice starts to soften. "But no. I have plans for you."

He pulls the gun out of my mouth, the aiming post knocking against my front teeth. I need to escape but there's nothing I can do. Jill must be a good distance away by now. They'll never catch her. That means he can kill me and I can still mark the mission as somewhat of a success. One casualty. Not bad. But God probably has something else in store for me. Either him or the devil.

Pa takes a step back, the fury in his eyes fades back to that cool and collected killing machine I know him to be. Now's my chance. I lunge forward. As my forehead drives at his nose, he leans back, just enough. I hit the fleshy protrusion and, following the laws of inertia, keep going until my forehead hits his lower jaw. Pain sears through my head. Skin rips. Teeth break away. He stumbles back, nose broken and mouth spewing blood.

"Fuck you!" He raises the gun.

Time slows.

One heartbeat.

Blood stings my eyes.

I close them.

The gun will be level with my head soon. He'll squeeze or jerk the trigger. A round will speed through the barrel. The pain in my head will explode and dissipate. I won't be coming back from this, not me. His revenge will only be mild compared with what he wants.

And I'll be dead.

Mindy will be alone. Mom will take care of her. The child will never know the father who loved her. Or maybe Pa will go after them, and my sacrifice will be for nothing.

The soft puffing sound of a weapon firing splits the air. I wait for the inevitable. Seconds pass. Blood flows freely from my forehead and down my cheeks. The metallic taste of copper fills my mouth.

How am I still alive?

He fired.

And I'm still here.

I crack one eye open. Pa lays on the ground in front of me, half his head blown away. Jill walks toward the body, AR 15 braced against her shoulder. She didn't run. Didn't take the easy way out. God love her.

She gets to Pa's body and nudges it a little with her foot, making sure he's dead. For good measure she empties the clip into him. His body bounces a little with the impacts. Her face stays flaccid as each bullet slams into the body.

"Fucking ass hole," she mutters. "Wanted to have me that one day before all this shit happened, and when I refused you decided to take me anyway. Used your connections to get me put in jail when I fought back. Looks good on you now, lying there all shot up." She spits on him. "You're lucky to get even that out of me."

She seems to see me for the first time. Her expression softens, lips go from a scorn to a slight smile but the corners tremble.

"Thanks," I say, waving toward Pa.

"Don't mention it." She slings the AR over her shoulder. "You okay?"

I want to laugh at what happened, cry out that I'm not okay, but there's still a lot of work left to do. A quick swallow forces back the shattered insides threatening exposure. "Yeah, it's just a flesh wound."

She must have known differently for she places a supporting hand is on my arm, then leads me to my ATV.

"We have a lot of driving to do. Think you can make it?"

"Sure." The world spins a little but steadies. "Just follow me and make sure I don't crash."

The landscape races by in a fog. Jill came up beside me a couple of times to jostle me back to the living. Red clouds my sight every few seconds but I brink it away.

Next thing I know someone is helping me up the stairs. Stripping off my clothes. Putting me to bed. And when I wake up in bed, one eye is covered and bandages are wrapped around my head.

Mindy sits next to me, her soft dark brown eyes asking the questions Jill probably wouldn't or couldn't answer – what did I do?

"Hi beautiful," I say, meaning every little bit of it. I want to run away with her. Someplace up north where corpses freeze and we don't have to worry about bikers. Don't think that's going to happen any time soon. It's going to be hard enough making sure our child lives past birth.

"Why do you have to do things the hard way?" she asks me, her eyes not wavering.

"For the challenge." I chuckle a little, but my head starts to pound.

"Don't try to do anything too fast, now. Doc came in and patched your forehead up but announced you'll soon look like Frankenstein's Monster if you keep this up."

"My head is killing me."

I reach up to rub it by she stops me, lowering my hand to my side. "If you saw what you looked like when you got home you wouldn't touch your head." The tips of her fingers gently touch my bandaged head. "You had a flap of skin hanging down and part of your skull was showing. Don't know what you did but I hope the other guy looks worse."

"He sure does." I try to sit up but she pushes me back. "Pa. We missed him with the first shot and he snuck up on me. I got some information out of him before head butting him. Broke his nose and took out a few teeth at the same time."

"That accounts for the wound." She takes her hand off my chest. "So, what did you find out?"

I take a deep breath. "They have a lot of women forced into being sex slaves at the house there. I want to get them out if we can."

"Always the bleeding heart," Jill says as she enters the room. "I was going to suggest that as well."

I hate bed rest. Not being able to move around makes me feel like an invalid, but I guess that's the idea. Make me want to ensure nothing like this happens again. Two days and I'm crawling the walls, but at least today I get to sit in with the group. Should be soon, they did say around five.

The first knock drifts upstairs and I swing out of bed, put on some pants. By the second knock I'm dressed and walking down to the living room. Jill is there with Carl. He looks good. Colour is back and he's standing well for someone shot just about two weeks ago. He smiles when I come down, crosses over, and gives me a hug. I return it, being careful not to squeeze too hard on his back.

Mindy, Cindy, Doc, Mom, Danny, Jill, Carl, and I take our seats at the table to discuss what we're going to do with the rest of The Family. We have no idea what to do at this point. The crap that hit the fan a couple of days ago should have quieted them down, but instead our people have seen them raiding just about anything they can get their hands on.

"If this keeps up they'll be in this area by next week," Danny says. "I flew over them yesterday and a bunch fanned out to follow me. The only advantage I have is not worrying about the terrain when flying." A smile breaks across her face. "Led a bunch of them into a herd."

The group chuckles.

"If they have sex slaves, then I say we kill them all," Jill says.

Cindy stares at the group. "They can't all be that bad."

"If one of them sits back and lets it happen then they're just as guilty," Mindy says.

They argue about this for a while, each putting forth their own opinion and then listening to the others. The headache starts to pound a little harder as each lets go of their frustration and desires. Carl seems to be doing the same as me, just listening and letting them talk it out.

What else are we going to do? We're on the injury list. It's times like this I feel useless and in need of more space to think.

"Why not just bomb them and do a raid?" I blurt out.

Danny laughs, but Mom cuts her off and leans forward.

"What do you mean?" She focuses on me.

"Well, we all think it's best if we rescue the women, right?"

They all agree readily.

I pick up steam. "We have access to multiple planes, one great pilot, and the ability to train a few others." One finger points in turn to Danny, myself, and Carl. He turns his head to stare at me for a minute. "We could make some more of those homemade bombs and load everyone up with some."

Mom barks a laugh. "Really? You think you could fly right now?"

"Not now, but maybe in a week." I point at Carl. "In one week you'll have both Carl and I ready to take on more stuff and we can group everyone together in order to build a little bit of a fighting force."

"The family has over two hundred bikers," Cindy says. "You sure we could take on all them?"

"I know we can." I look from one to the other. "Carl is great with mechanical, so we put him in charge of fixing up some of the planes at the airport. Mom, you have tactics and know how to make a good attack plan and build the bombs just like you did a while ago. Danny, you could have some of us up and running with aviation in no time. Jill, I bet you'd make a good pilot. And Mindy, you get to stay home and grow our little devil."

10

LET'S GO SHOPPING

Mom and I walk to the big shed on the property. It's where she kept everything needed to run the camp. Now she keeps the ATVs under the awning with a bank of solar chargers. Most of us faced the issue of paying for skyrocketing electric bills or going off the grid. A lot of us chose off the grid because we knew the price of electricity had only one way to go.

Three solar banks angled south reflect sunlight. Three ATVs sit connected to their charging units. Crisp air blows across the tree tops and some of it actually gets down to us. Such a beautiful late May day. Hard to believe how much has happened in a few weeks. Wispy clouds decorate the sky this morning, perfect for flying, but that's not what's happening today. It's inventory and shopping day. Need to make a bomb? Well, got no better teacher than my mom. Most kids learned how to do a lot of things with their parents. Not me, survival, hunting, and a lot of tactics training went into my childhood. You'd think they wanted me to be a soldier or something. Too bad I became a tech instead. Must have been a real disappointment to them.

I carry the notepad because my writing is easier to read than hers. A simple necessity. She doesn't realize I'm the one going on the shopping spree. It's going to be a fight, but I need her to deflect Mindy from thinking she's going. No need to put her in harm's way. I'm taking Jill with me; she's the closest thing to a back watcher as I can get since Carl is still laid up from the gunshot. Doc says he should be able to get on his feet full-time in another week or so.

Jill is concerned. She confessed Carl won't let himself heal. Keeps trying to do things like move heavy stuff around when she's not there. I had a talk with him last night, made him promise to not do anything because I'll need his help in the future. He grudgingly agreed. Jill will let me know if he tries anything, in case I need to smack him around.

"Fertilizer, ammonium nitrate based, the key word is nitrate." Mom opens the door to the storage area in the shed. One fertilizer bag sits there. "Need at least four bags."

"Got it. About five kilos?"

"Yes, but tell them to get six just in case." She steps into the room. "Need something to contain the mixture but not too strong to decrease the explosion."

"Plastic bottles, like water bottles with the water poured out. Lots of them out there."

She seems to stare at nothing for a few seconds. "Go into Canadian Tire if possible. They always have a lot of bottled water in cases. Pick up two – no three cases of twenty-four. We'll drain and dry them. Nothing but tap water anyway."

"Good, that puts us in the same store for the fertilizer as well. What else?"

"Don't want to use gas, most of it has gone bad unless we find treated stuff. Get a couple of jerry cans, four litres. If you find fuel stabilizer then pick up a lot of that if possible. Also fuel line conditioner, it'll help remove water from the gas if need be." Her gaze rests on a shelf. "Kerosene. Get as much as you can. Stuff like naphtha will do the trick. It stays good longer than the other stuff and works just as fine for what it'll be used for."

"We'll need something other than the ATVs to bring all this back."

"And more than two people." She turns to me. "Look, I know you want to do this raid, and I can't think of anyone else who can do it better than you. Hell, you'll have a bunch of good people volunteering to go with you." Mom takes a deep breathe.

Something she's not saying makes the hairs on the neck stand. "But what?"

"But nothing. I would ask Carl to go but he's got a hole in his back that's not healed yet." She turns back to the stock room. "Mindy's going to be a pain in my ass with this raid."

"You bet."

"I don't want her to go with you." Mom turns back to me. "I can't stomach her getting killed in a raid like this. I know she's strong, but she's also carrying my grandchild and it shows. That time on the container took a lot out of both of them."

Not sure what she's getting at, so I take a stab in the dark. "You think something's wrong with the pregnancy?"

"Well, if you don't think so as well then there's something wrong with your observational skills, and I didn't take all that time to teach you to be observant without it sinking in."

I think back to this morning and what the sheets looked like. "You mean the blotting, right?"

"Yes, the blotting. The small tell-tale signs of something going wrong. Blood stains, if you will. I told Doc to take a good look at her. He's up there now."

I nod, the small knot of tension flows out of me. "We don't have much here to figure it out. Doc was a vet, you know."

She smiles at me. "I know. Hell, I almost grabbed him when people started to show up, but some of your group were there that day. Didn't want them to know we existed." She squats on her haunches. "We need some type of fuse."

"Timed or lit?"

"I'd love a timed one, lit is probably what we'll end up using. Going to be hell to light in the plane, and we need to be able to adjust the timing…"

Her eyes glass over. She's thinking, and that's always a good sign when we have a small problem. My mom can outwit just about anyone and think her way out of any situation when she puts her mind to it. Give her a problem and soon she'll come up with a solution. As the smile starts to creep across her face I know we're good.

"Get soap as well."

I write it down. "We need people to start bathing regular or something?"

"Not really, they try to do that all the time here. Well's deep you know. Try being on the road and seeing what you smell like after a few days." She points to the list. "Make sure the soap is a glycerine base, not a moisturizing one."

My pen is flying, but my curiosity is begging to know why. "I don't understand the difference."

"It's time to make napalm."

The cube van sits in the north field with a few discarded boat hulls. Each of the small frames mark another experiment gone wrong from my youth as I tried to figure out what I wanted to do with my life. An engineer, a mechanic, a welder. Each tells a different story.

But the van is not one of my experiments in life. It's the thing that will help us get what we need. I open the door, climb in, insert the key, and give it a quarter turn. The dash lights up and a chime tries to remind me the door is open. The only thing I'm worried about is the gas gauge. The fuel light comes on and the small readout on the dash says ten kilometres until empty. Where the hell am I going to get gas for this thing? Nearest place would be Aurora Road and forty-eight, but is there still gas there, and is it still good? These are things I need to think about right now. Two stations with different types of holding tanks. I'll need a long hose with a pump.

I can use the van's battery to power the pump, not a problem there, but I'll need a length of hose to put into the submerged tanks. Getting the caps off is another issue. There's going to be a lot of noise. And with noise comes corpses. They're drawn to anything disturbing the peace and quiet. I watched one follow a flock of ducks for several minutes as they flew south. And any time we shoot something, they're sure to show up. There needs to be another way.

"Looking for a way to fuel up?"

I about die. Didn't even hear him approach. "Fuck Carl, do I need to put a bell around your neck?"

He laughs, then winces. There's still pain. He should be in bed.

"I knew you'd be looking at everything before going out, and I'm bored. Jill won't let me do anything."

"Take it from someone who's been shot before, you want to rest. Heal. I need you, so do a lot of people around here. Anyway, Jill won't forgive me if anything happened to you."

"You need around five volts DC." He leans against the van. "There's a little bit of a trick to it, but attaching the van battery to the actual pump will allow you to drive up, fill up, and get on your way as if you paid at the pump."

"First time I've heard this, explain."

He goes over it for me. Take the face plate off the pump, locate some wires, use a regulator to step down the voltage of the battery, then pump. Simple, but where the hell to find the regulator?

"Use the one in the van," he says.

I must be wearing my stupid face.

Carl sighs. "Look, most of the electronics in this thing are low voltage, like five volts." He reaches in and pulls off an access cover. "See the fuses? Locate the one going to the dash and you have a five volt line in there. Tap into that and you can run the pump without any issues. Got it?"

I sigh. "Well, I can probably figure it out in a pinch but I'm no mechanic."

"Okay, you'll need someone to do it for you then. Got any ideas?" He stands there, grinning.

"Oh no you don't." I pull the keys out of the ignition and step out of the van. "I see what you're doing. I'll tell Jill about it."

"Don't doubt you will."

"And she'll have a lot to say about your injured ass in the van while we do our shopping."

"Wouldn't think otherwise." He's still grinning.

"So what makes you think she'll let you get away with it?"

"Because there's no one else who knows how to do it."

Jill stares at me from across the table in Mom's dining room. She's trying to kill me with her eyes, I can tell. The rest of the pack is sitting at the table, Mom, Carl, Doc, Cindy, Danny, and Mindy. I laid out the plan with Carl there so no one would think it was his idea. Heck, maybe that would have been better, tell them there's no more gas in the van and let Carl make the suggestion. Unfortunately, that's not how I roll. Maybe the tanks are empty; maybe the gas is really bad. I don't know. Crap, I'm surprised we've lasted this long, but what else can you do?

"I'm going," Carl says to the group. "Two things you don't know about. One, I'm the only person who knows how to wire the van into the pump and bypass the system inside the station that keeps the thing from pumping. Two, I know how to clear the gas and help bring it back. Any of you know how to mix ethanol into the system and what to look out for?" He glances around at the blank faces. "Of course not, but that's how we do it."

Jill shakes her head. "I don't want you to go. You're not healed."

"Actually, he is well healed," Doc says. "Just a matter of the muscles knitting together a little more."

Jill glares at the man. "You're not helping." She faces Carl again, face flushed. "Look, if something happens you'll need to get back here and we all know how fast you can run right now."

"Not very, but when do things really go wrong?" Carl says.

"All the time," I say. "Look, Carl. I think the best thing is we bring you along for the gas, but after that you come back to camp."

Jill still stares at me, but at lease she's not trying to kill me.

I take another shot. "So, if we get him back to camp before anything happens can he come with us?"

Jill stands. Her finger jabs at me with each word. "You better make sure that promise is kept."

The van's engine turns with a chug. Carl is sitting on one of the ATVs watching as we try to coax the thing to life.

"Try again but don't flood it. Don't give it gas," Carl says.

I turn the ignition again. The starter engages and tries to turn the engine but nothing happens besides chugging. Crestfallen, I let go of the key. "What's wrong with it?"

"Charlie will probably know better than me. We need to get him over here."

"He's been out hunting since yesterday. Something about deer." I glance at the dash. Battery's almost dead. "Any way to kick this thing into starting?"

Carl gets off the ATV. "We could try something, but don't complain if it backfires. Pop the hood."

I do so and Carl disappears behind the metal barrier. He tinkers in there for a while and I just wait, drumming my fingers on the steering wheel as if a light needs to change. After a few moments rhe pulls the hood down and steps back.

"Try now."

I give the engine a turn, it chugs again, tries to start, then catches and revs to life.

"What'd you do?"

Carl holds up a small bottle of clear liquid. "Ethanol. Best thing for vans that won't start." He heads to the ATV. "We'll need a lot more of it for the gas when we pull it up. The stuff will work in a vehicle, but after a short time it will rot the seals and gaskets. This is a Hail Mary sort of play."

"Okay, we'll pick up Jill and make our way to the station. You following?"

Carl sits on the ATV. "Nope, going to meet you up there."

I lean out the window. "That's not the plan."

"Yeah, but I need to get some wind in my hair before I'm back in bed for another week. This is about as much freedom as I can get with Jill around." He takes off, waving to me over his back. I don't want to be in his shoes when Jill gets a hold of him. Hell, I don't want to be in my shoes right now, but something has to be done.

I slam the van into gear and drive to the cottages. Jill's standing there with her bow slung over her shoulder and a quiver full of arrows. Nice to see she remembers. She opens the door and jumps in. "Where's Carl?"

Okay, time to die. "He took off ahead of us."

She looks ahead and utters one word. "Drive."

I'm a dead man. So is Carl when she gets to him.

The small town the camp is near was cleared out of corpses by Mom and the group a while ago. It's not saying some didn't find their way onto the streets at some point, but not many. We head up Ninth Line and turn on Aurora Road, heading for the two stations. Carl's got to be there already. His head start was just enough to make sure of that. Jill keeps giving me the cold shoulder as we drive.

Carl is at the station on the north side of the road, not the one at the corner. He's got a pump taken apart and ready for us, but he has a lot of sweat on his brow. I pull up making sure the passenger side is facing the pump. No need to have the filler on the wrong side. I pop the hood and turn off the engine, hoping it will start after filling up.

Two wires are attached to the pump and the van, and Carl is able to get the thing working.

I open the door and get out. "Why this one?"

"Further away from the road and the station sees less traffic than the other one. This means less air in the tanks and thus, less moisture. Better gas."

"Makes sense."

Jill climbs out of the van, walks to Carl, and starts talking in a hushed voice. I climb out and walk to the other gas station, not wanting to hear the dressing down my friend is receiving. You'd think Carl would know what Jill's response would be from that brain-dead manoeuvre but it seems he either doesn't or just refuses to care. The other gas station is situated on the corner and I head to it. They have a well-stocked store inside with a lot of storage compared to the one Carl picked, but I can understand why he went after the one he did. I'm looking for something special to take back to Mindy.

Once in the store, I scan the place before prying open the doors. The stench of death hits me and a couple of corpses lying on the ground with heads blown off tell me why. Not a lot of light enters the area but I can still see. Any sealed food is a good bet, as long as the package isn't blown. I stay away from the coolers, nothing in there will be worth taking. Chips, pop, beef jerky, stuff like that is what I look for. I pile everything on the counter. There's the special fudge but it's all mouldy. Hard candies in wrappers stick out like decorations on a Christmas tree. I pull out three cases. Looks like she's going to get spoiled today.

Not thinking, I walk behind the counter looking for a plastic bags. A rotted corpse with its head blown clean off lays sprawled with a shotgun to the side. I pick up the weapon, put it on the counter, and start bagging my spoils. Movement outside catches my eye and I stop shoving things in bags. A few corpses walk along the road toward the station. Maybe not right at the station, but close enough that they'll see me. I finish packing away my find and head for the door, keeping low. A glance outside and I'm out the door, heading to the van. Carl and Jill are still talking, but it looks like the situation has settled down.

I shove the bags into the van. "We filled yet?"

"Just gotta put the ethanol into the tank," Carl says.

"Make it fast. We've got company."

Both of them look up as corpses start to enter the intersection.

Jill stares at them. "Shit."

11

WALKING WITH CORPSES

Corpses don't move fast, they just never stop. It seems the only thing that can stop them is destroying the brain or putting something impassible between you and them like a barrier or steep hill. We only have the van. Yes, it is large, but we need to have it moving and don't want to make it an obstacle.

Jill jumps into the cab and I slide in behind the wheel real quick. Carl is finishing off dumping a jug of ethanol into the tank, and I hope what's in the system is enough to get us started. The contents of the tank will mix as we drive, or that's my hope.

Jill sticks her head out. "Finish it up!"

"Carl!" I call out. Corpses lumber around the corner, not more than fifty metres away. Damn they're getting close.

"Just a little more." Carl keeps dumping ethanol.

"It doesn't have to be perfect. We got enough." I push the keys into the ignition and twist. The starter tries to turn over the engine. "Shit, come on. Not now."

"We may need to dump some into the intake. Pop the hood," Carl says as he steps in front of the van.

I twist the ignition again. "No, go!"

"It's no good if you don't get out to the stores. Pop the hood. I'm going to stand here until you do, so might as well get it over with."

Fucking hard-headed trucker. I want to beat him regardless of how I feel about him, but he has a point. We have to get the van started and he's the one who can get it done with the small amount left if the jug. I pull the release.

The hood goes up and Carl gets to work. A few seconds pass. Corpses get closer. They've covered half the distance now. More round the intersection following the leaders.

I hit the horn. "Enough already!"

The hood drops and Carl motions for me to try again. The engine catches, revs up, and backs down to normal.

He rushes from in front of the van. "Now get out of here! I'll see you back at camp."

I drop the van into gear and slam on the gas. It lumbers forward at a good speed but I'm not trying to be an Indie driver, only need enough momentum up to make it through the crowd coming toward us. We hit them at forty. Corpses crash against the front of the van and slam to the ground. Others reach up at the windows with hands like claws. I don't know how many I run over, but at times the wheels spin and I'm scared we'll get stuck.

The wall of corpses thin, then we're out of them, driving down an open road.

We pass the wholesale Housing and storage place, there's only two of the homes left of their lot. Someone has scavenged them. I keep going, not worrying about who could be doing what. As we approach Stouffville Road, cars litter the intersection, just as they were when I took Mindy into town a lifetime ago. Nothing has changed. A corpse is still in one of the cars, clawing at the window. The white bones of its hands have raked all the grime and blood off the inside of the car.

It was last year we left the corpse there, hoping a cure or something would come to reverse the situation in our world, but there's nothing. I glance at over to Jill, she's shaking her head. No time to be kind to those not pursing us. It affords me time to look down Main Street and see what's happening to the small town of Stouffville. Once, it was hard to call it a small town. The population exploded with those moving away from the city to have a life outside of Toronto. They wanted to get away from the crime and greed. Only, when they moved into the town they realized something else put a divide between the locals and them. The hockey society, holier-than-thou attitudes, and an entitled belief system of the older class of people in town. Homes more expensive than their Toronto counterparts filled the realtor walls and people unable to buy them went into hock for the privilege to live in the area.

Now, the deserted streets hold nothing but a few broken down vehicles and corpses staggering around. Hopefully the sound of this noisy van that tilts and wavers down the road will not attract them. Only close ones turn toward us and I count our luck for such an occurrence.

We turn onto Hoover Park Drive and then into the Smart Centre. The Crappy Tire is there with a bunch of other retail stores and a Walley Mart that dwarfs any retail outlet nearby. The land it takes up is easily twice the size of Crappy Tire. Corpses mill around outside it like the living used to do, only this time they're not looking for their cars.

"I don't understand it," Jill says.

"Understand what?"

"Why they're all gathered around over there."

I take us on a looping way to the Canadian Tire store, keeping our speed low and noise to a minimum. "It could be anything. Maybe deep down they realize this was part of a past life. A place they want or need to be. A memory of something better. Or maybe they sense that this is where people go for food and that's why they're there."

"It's creepy." Jill rolls up her window. "Let's get in and out as fast as possible."

"I'll agree to that."

I bring us to a halt outside the garden centre of Crappy Tire. It's the farthest away from the biggest group of milling corpses, and most everything we want will be there. The fence is not high and Jill spots an unlocked gate. We both head to it, wanting to be quiet.

Inside there's a trolley we can use to put stuff on, that makes our exposure to the open wilds less, and allows me a little more happiness.

It makes a little wobbling noise as I push it, but nothing loud enough to gain watching eyes. We pile six bags of fertilizer on the thing, making sure they're a nitrate base.

The doors to the main store are another issue. They're closed, but not locked. I try pushing and pulling to no avail. It takes both Jill and I a concerted effort to pry them apart and slide them into the store. Smart but dumb, that's what Mindy calls me. Sliding doors are the bane of my existence.

Little light comes into the store. The dimness adds that special creep factor to what we're doing and sweat builds on my forehead. The odour of decay and death hangs in the air. Both of us pull our bows out and nock an arrow. I take my time pushing the trolley through the store. No need to make a mess of things or attract attention.

Jill's bow twangs as she lets fly an arrow. She has another one nocked just as quick. Stumbling echoes through the store and a crash of something large falling against pots.

"I'm an idiot," I whisper.

Jill keeps scanning the store. "What?"

"When Mindy and I raided this place last year we propped open a loading bay door in case we needed to get back in."

"Propped it up? You mean left it open for more corpses to walk in here?"

I shake my head. "No, left enough room for someone to put their hands under it and lift the thing."

"Wouldn't that make a lot of noise?"

"You're right. Good thing I didn't remember it."

She lets fly another arrow. We're nearer to the check out lane now, making our way to the camping supplies. "Didn't your Mom want glycerine soap?"

"Yeah, why?"

Jill takes off down an aisle and returns carrying four large packs. "On sale over there." She nods to where she loosed the arrow. "Trying to save money, you know." There's the wink. Jill is back.

"Good, don't think I have a lot of room on the card." I smile.

We have the soap, fertilizer, and all we need to get is the naphtha. As we pass the cash, I reach out and snag a pack of lighters.

"Don't you think she would have one?"

I hold one up, a windless lighter. Guaranteed to work even when wet.

"You're getting to be too smart for your britches there, Steve."

We get to the camping area and place ten two litre cans of naphtha on the trolley and make our way back. It's a good thing Mindy and I basically cleared this place out of corpses a year ago. Hard to tell why there's more in here now, but it's always best not to dwell on the mysteries.

The door to outside is a little bit away but something is wrong. No sound. The air is too quiet. No birds like there was earlier. There's a strange tinge to the atmosphere. Shadows dance on the ground. Corpses hover around. Once at the door, I can see a whole lot of them milling about the van. There's no way we have enough arrows for them, and if we used guns, the other's in the parking lot outside Wal-Mart would be here in not time. We're screwed.

"Now what?" Jill asks.

"Let me think," I say. Fucked is all I can come up with. I start to pace, rubbing the back of my neck and shaking my head. "Corpses around the van probably came from the Wal-Mart parking lot. That place was packed and nothing we can do about moving them out of the way. If we distract the ones around the van then we may attract the ones in that parking lot. We need to get something around the corner that will pull them over to that side of the smart centre without causing much grief here.

"Jill, do you know where the vice grips are in the store?"

"Think so, why?"

"Grab a big pair and meet me at the loading dock, I got an idea." Shit, I hope this works.

She takes off into the store and I run toward automotive. The guys always keep an air compressor for people with no air in their tires in the parking lot. It's there, no battery charge but the cylinder is full, all fifteen gallons of it. I start looking for an impact wrench and a large metal can along with twine. Both are right where I thought they should be and I head to the loading dock.

Jill is nocking an arrow as I approach, a corpse is on the ground.

"Took your time. Had to remove three of these things before coming in." She hands me the vice grips. "So, what's the plan?"

"I'm taking this stuff to the other side of WalMart."

She stares at me blankly. "You going to ask them to bring their cars for a free tire rotation or something?"

"No, but do you think that would work?" I smile. "Here." I hand her the line and wrap twine around the trigger of the impact wrench. Next, I tighten the vice grip over its nib.

Jill scratches her head. "I still don't get it."

"Easy. I put the wrench in the garbage can and attach the air hose. It rattles like a son-of-a-bitch and draws them all away. We then load the van and take off." I hand her the keys. "When this goes off I'll run back inside and make sure the last of it gets into the van, if you haven't gotten everything."

She stares at the keys. "If I don't bring you back, Mindy will skin me alive."

"If I don't come back, Mindy will find a way to bring me back and then kill me," I say. "Anyway, unless you know how to do this, it's up to me. I want to make the biggest impact on the ones outside the door here, so maybe I'll put it out front of the shop or something."

"That's better than running with all that to the other side of Wal-Mart, but what makes you think it'll work?"

"They're attracted to sound, right?"

She nods. "Okay, better get started before I change my mind on this." Jill gives me a kiss on the cheek. "For luck."

I blush a little. She's like the sister I never had. Damn happy we found her when we did last year and rescued her this year. Feels like a habit, rescuing people. We're doing this so we can rescue a bunch of women I've never met, and before that I would do anything to help out others. Looks like what Mom and Dad drilled into me as a kid stuck.

"See you in a bit," I say, and open the back door.

The late afternoon sun beats down making me wonder if we're going to have as hot a summer as last year when all this happened. Will the corpses migrate up and then back? The mean temperature in

Ontario is good for them, so maybe that'll happen. We can start living in peace as we thin the heard on its travels back and forth.

I walk to where the auto shop is and stop. There are a few corpses milling around. I take out my bow and nock an arrow, six left. Better make all of them count. I drop three without problems but the fourth is behind a car. Fuck it. I pull the compressor to the front of the store and put the metal garbage can down. The hose attaches to the impact wrench easily enough and I check the vice grip on the bit end. Probably should have used an air chisel but I can't think of everything. It goes into the can and I place the contraption on the ground. I start to hook the hose up to the compressor but hesitate. This needs to be loud enough to attract them, but not too loud to get the whole horde in the parking lot over here. We may need to do this type of run again.

Settling in my mind what needs to happen, I dispense with the make shift plan and pull something else out of my ass, and I don't think it's my head. I walk to the front doors, moving slow to avoid attention. When I'm there, I see Jill staring at me from the other door. She has her hands out and she's shrugging. Probably thinks I'm an idiot. Not my place to tell her she's wrong.

I walk near the front of the van and get a few metres away from a corpse. The thing finally lifts its gaze and sees me. Its mouth opens and closes methodically. One eye is missing from its face, probably due to the huge gash there. It takes one step forward, rotted legs jerking as if they fight the command to move. At two metres I start to back up and snap my fingers. The other corpses look up and start to follow as well. It's working. They're drawn to the noise but the ones in the WalMart parking lot are oblivious to it. This is going to work. A quick glance behind shows the others are not coming, only the ones from the van.

"Come on, boys. Look at this. Don't worry about the van. Nothing to see there."

Jill is out of the store and loading the van. She keeps glancing at me as if worried. Nothing to worry about, Jill. I have this under control.

"Look at the nice, walking, side of beef here. You know you want it. Come get it."

There's ten of them following me now. I keep ahead of them not wanting any to catch me due to something stupid. Most of the time I'm walking sideways, making sure I keep an eye on them and the ones in the WalMart parking lot. The side of the building comes up faster than I imagine. The corpses are actually walking at a good pace. A little farther and we'll be there. I'll run for the door when I round the corner and I know the corpses are following me.

A few more metres to go.

"Come on you guys, keep up."

One of the corpses slows as if it's having second thoughts about dinner.

"Over here!" I say a little louder. "Nothing to eat over there but a metal van. I'm flesh and bone."

It turns back, missing Jill as she loads the last of the naphtha into the van. Not much further to go.

I round the corner and a cold hand reaches out. It's the one from the auto shop. The bugger did see me but took its time coming out. A gaping maw descend on me. Feted breathe fills my nose with vile scents, and milky white eyes glare at me. There's no anger, no hate, only a desire to eat, and I'm the one on the main course. The nails on the fingers are sharp and they scratch at me. I pull an arrow out and strike, but only get it into the back, well below the brain. Another attempt, then another. Soon all I can think of is getting the arrow into the brain of the corpse. Nothing else is around me but that one fiend.

Finally, with a last desperate stab, the eyes roll and mouth stops chomping. The arrow is in its brain.

I look over to see the other ten still coming, not stopping. The whole fight only lasted a second or two, but the other corpses didn't stop to watch, why would they? They're just as hungry and don't tire or become curious about an outcome. They want to feed.

One gets my foot and the other a handful of shirt. I'm forced down as fingers pull dead bodies toward the exposed flesh of my face. My heart pounds. Desperation takes hold of my. I have a few arrows but there's three of them on me. Another seven are coming this way. This is the end I didn't expect, smothered by creatures eating my flesh. Not the right way to go. Mindy will cry. She won't know what to do after I'm gone. Hopefully Mom will help her. Maybe train the little one when I'm dead and tell him or her about me. That would be nice. At least both Jill and Carl will make it home. I would hate to have their lives on my head as well.

The first one is right there in my face. I reach up and grab its throat, try to squeeze. Flesh parts but muscle is still there trying to obey the commands of an inactive brain. It leans into the hold, hands with sharp nails raking down my arms until blood spatters across my vision.

12

ONE GOOD DEED

The broken teeth in the corpse's mouth descend on me like crows on road kill. Mindy's going to kill me for this. My child is going to grow up without a father. Hopefully Mom or one of my friends will step up and help with the job of instilling the right things to do or say. Protection for the kid is my only concern.

The jaws don't bite down. The struggle to reach my flesh stops and dead weight leans in on me. I open one eye enough to see through it. The corpse is still there, mouth open, but not moving. An arrow sticks out of the back of its skull. I look to the left. Jill stands there, arrow nocked and firing at a horde of corpses lumbering toward us. She saved me. Again. Guess saving her last year is finally paying off. I push the corpse off me.

The lumbering bodies get closer. There's so many of them, more than one can count when you're facing them from the ground. There could be hundreds, or thousands, making their way toward us. We need to get out of there.

"Thanks," I struggle to say. The corpse rolls off me. They all have arrows sticking out of their heads at odd angles.

"Get off your ass, will you. I'm running out of arrows, and when that happens the AR comes out. That'll bring the whole bunch down on us." Jill pulls another arrow out and lets it loose on the nearest corpse. It falls. She's really gotten good with that thing.

"I'm up," I say, feet now under me. The world spins and bile threatens to race up my throat but I shake hard to get rid of it. "Let's get to the van." I pull out my Glock, check the chamber, and disengage the safety. "How many arrows do you have left?"

The bark of the AR sounds. "None."

Fuck, if some of them hung back, this will convince them to come. Nothing says dinner bell to a corpse like firing a riffle without a suppressor.

I run to the van, look out to the road, a wall of corpses move toward us. They're not that close but like I said in the past, what they lack in speed they make up for in stamina. Not one of them will stop until they reach their goal, and right now that's Jill and me.

The keys are inside the van. That annoying beep hammers at my ears when I open the door. Thank God Jill didn't take them with her. I give the thing a quarter turn, making sure it primes the engine before pushing it over to start. The flywheel chugs and finally the engine catches.

"We're out of here!"

She lowers the AR and rushes to the passenger side. The door opens smoothly to her yank and she's in the van, panting. "Let's go!"

I shove the gear selector into drive as Jill releases the clip and jams another into the rifle. She rams the charger and the weapon is hot again. Time to rock and roll.

The gas pedal goes down and we move forward at breathtaking velocity. In other words, a snail's pace. The van is great for hauling stuff but not so great for speed or acceleration. A kid on a tricycle could beat us off the line. Probably for the first half kilometre as well. But what we lack in get up and go we make up for in inertia. We're taking corpses out as they claw and try to get at us. At times the tires spin and we slip a little sideways on the smears left behind, but we keep going. Once around the east side of Crappy Tire I gun toward the road, then onto forty-eight.

Jill glances at me, scanning. "Are you bit?"

"No, why?"

"Then why are you taking this route?"

"Time to thin the herd a little."

"Just turn onto Hoover Park and get out of their way."

Good idea, but I'm feeling vengeance well up in me for all the lives the corpses have taken.

"Sure, and when they fill up Stouffville with all their milling about you can thank yourself for the problems of getting shitter paper from the GT Boutique." I try to smile at her, but it just won't come.

"Shit," she whispers.

"Exactly," I respond.

"Okay, let's take them out if we can." She braces herself against the dash. "Fast and deadly or methodical?"

If we go fast then the chances of getting overwhelmed are slim, but then again, you hit anything fast enough no matter how light or soft it is you'll get damaged. Better to take a chance than risk it. We need to get these supplies to the camp.

"We'll hit them at fifty and turn onto Stouffville Road. That'll pull a lot of them out of town and away from where we're going." I try to remember the roads but there's no need. Most of them are either north south or east west. "Turn onto McCowan and then take Bloomington over."

"Sounds good." Jill rolls her window down a little.

"What're you doing?"

"Target practice."

"We don't have the ammo to waste."

She pouts and rolls the window back up. "I'm thinking we'll need to add some long cutting blades to the side of the van. That way if this happens again we can take a bunch of them out."

"Sounds good. Our next stop is finding a fuel pump so we can pull diesel out of the underground tanks."

"Why diesel?"

"Doesn't degrade like gas does." I push the van a little and it chugs, like the gas is really bad and full of water. "Diesel will last a number of years, you just have to strain it, according to Carl. Best idea yet and there's a lot of those trucks sitting around. And they don't take a lot of maintenance."

The lead corpse hits the grill. I turn my attention back to the road, looking for a route through the bodies that isn't as packed as the others. No such luck. The mob is thick and the van keeps mowing them over. The thing is going to look gruesome. Blood and bits of body start to cake the window and I use the wipers, but they don't clear as much as smear it. I can't see very well so put on the washer fluid. It helps until one corpse grabs a wiper blade and it comes off in its grip. Fuck. Only one left but at least we're almost at the road.

We're down to thirty so I try to give it more gas only to get a heavier chug out of the van. Even with all we did the gas is still bad. "Come on!"

"Why are you slowing down?"

"Not trying to, it's happening. The gas is bad and nothing is getting us up the hill."

We only have a little more to go until we're over the hill and able to use gravity to help push us the rest of the way home. It's not helping that the corpses are slowing us down by pure numbers. There seems to be no end to the amount of them walking this road. It's like they packed together to find food or warmth. Who knows what goes through their heads. Every indication is they only do two things, eat and walk. And where everything they eat goes, I don't know.

We're over the small hill and on our way down. The van is not picking up speed but neither is it slowing. I need to get us clear of the corpses. If the gas was good, this would have been a great plan, but the engine is struggling to get through the moisture mixed in with the fuel. This is not a good batch, and we're in trouble, more than I want to admit.

"There needs to be something I can do," Jill says.

"Get out and push if you don't mind."

"I could shoot a few of the ones in front."

I shake my head. "You'd have to lean out too far to do it with the AR. The ones at the side will be able to reach you." I glance at the speedometer; we're almost at thirty again. "We're picking up a little speed. Not a lot, but enough. We'll make it."

Stouffville Road is ahead but the wall of corpses hasn't let up. I need to slow a little to make the turn and apply the brakes. At twenty I swerve into the oncoming lane, add a little gas, and pray that hitting them sideways will afford us less resistance. As we make the last part of the turn, some of the ethanol must hit the engine for it chugs to life with enthusiasm. We shoot to forty and the speed keeps climbing as the corpses are left behind.

I breathe, not realizing I held my breath for a while there.

Jill touches my arm. "You can slow down now." There's a rattling under the cab. "Think something is broke so take your time getting us home."

The entrance to the golf course passes by. It registered as a short cut to me but I let it pass, not knowing how large the herd is. Something tells me the masses from up north have joined the Toronto group and are now traveling together. If that's so, they could be miles long and millions in numbers. The thought makes me shake.

McCowan Road comes up and I turn onto it. The use of roads makes sense, little obstructions and it's more even for traveling. They probably funnelled to the flat surface. We need to do something about that, clear them out somehow.

Bethesda passes by and the engine is back to chugging. At least we're not battling through corpses so we're able to keep a good speed. We really need something new to get the women out of Uxbridge and maybe rid the town of the bikers.

We hit Bloomington Road and I make a right. The high impact intersection up ahead is no worries, don't have to wait for the light. As we hit the top of the hill I slow and come to a stop. Both Jill and I stare out at the sea of corpses making their way through the intersection. We're not going this way.

I turn us around, head back to McCowan, and point us north. We get to Aurora Road and find the same wall of corpses making their way south. Too many of them to plough through. Anyway, having them follow us back to camp is not an option I need to think about. If that many came in, they would surely set off some of the traps and the resulting explosions would bring even more. It's time to rethink the defence of our home.

Back to McCowan we go, this time to Vivian Road. Once there, it is clear to cross but instead I turn us south on forty-eight.

Jill grabs my arm. "What the fuck are you doing?"

"We need to find out where they end." I wave in the direction where we came, while we creep down the road at a safe twenty, hoping to see them before they see or hear us. We get to the church and I see the next hill down the road in the distance. It's covered with corpses. And by the time we're another hundred metres the full extent is there before us, the line must stretch ten kilometres. I had thought hundreds or even thousands. It comes to mind we are talking about millions of corpses making their way south. This is not good if someone is still alive down there. Hell, this is not good if someone is still alive up here when they turn around and head north for the summer.

We roll into camp grim with news. The group gathers around us as we come to a stop and exit. My back is sore from the ride and I need to stretch it out. The van is not the most comfortable vehicle by a long shot. The park comes alive as we roll up the back to display our findings. Mindy is there and I hand over the bag of goodies. She immediately goes for the spicy corn chips and hands the rest of the bag over to the others. The best treats are shared treats.

Charlie and Carl do a walk around the van after I tell them what happened. Danny comes over and starts talking with them. They get me to pop the hood and the three of them whistle. Guess it looks a lot worse than it is.

Mom gets several of the younger guys to take the water bottles to Shadow Pond, the little body of water beside Shadow Lake. It's not large, just what we call the thing. She wants them to empty the water into the pond and bring the plastic empties back. Should take them a while and gets us some alone time with the adults.

"There's a wall of corpses making their way North. Not sure how many, but they covered a lot of the road." I keep explaining what we saw on our way back and Carl comes over with Charlie, they're carrying an arm. In the hand is a wiper assembly, the one we lost.

"This was bouncing in the engine compartment. Lucky it didn't hit anything," Charlie says.

Jill points to the wiper. "Can you put it back on?"

"I don't think it's worth it," I say. "The gas was really bad and the ethanol only helped a little. Think we need to go after a diesel like you suggested there, Carl."

Both he and Charlie nod.

"Time to retire her," Charlie says. "She did us well for the time, but now she's no good."

"What about Betsy?" Danny motions to her plane. "Is all the gas bad?"

"Most of it," Carl says. "We're lucky to have gotten as much out of it as we did. Maybe we can change the engine over to ethanol and brew a bunch up for you."

"Sounds like a good idea," Danny says. "But what are we going to use to get the still going?"

I give her a little smile. "All we need is an orchard or farm."

Everything is put into the storage area, and we really need to get things going, but lunch is lunch, and both Jill and I are hungry after our morning run. It only takes a few minutes to convince both of us to take the time and refuel our bodies.

Mom's homemade bread is the best you can get. Soft and moist, heavy and willing to suck up anything you put it into. The only thing we have to do that with is canned gravy we got from a raid last week. I don't care, it's enough to make me want to wolf the whole thing down, and I do. Half a loaf and a full can later I'm standing there looking at what Jill and I pulled out of Crappy Tire. Enough to hopefully make some bombs for Mom.

"The first thing we need to do is grind up the soap," Mom says. "That way we can dissolve it in the naphtha."

I'm still a little puzzled at this, and when I'm puzzled I ask a lot of questions. "What will that do?"

"Napalm," Mom says. "One of the best things to come out of the Korean conflict of the sixties."

Jill looks up from examining the haul. "How do you know all this?"

Mom gives her a sideways look. "Even now I'm supposed to be silent, but I guess nothing will come of it if I say something. Remember, the Government has ears everywhere."

I laugh. "Sure, and the corpses are part of the Government's plan to thin the herd and let us become a smaller nation again."

"You laugh now, but wait until Ottawa resurfaces." Mom hands over a grater. "Now, start breaking the bars down and don't get anything else in the mix."

The three of us start grating, turning the glycerine soap into crumbs. It's hard work, making my hand muscles cramp as the soap turns into power. We get a pail done and Mom dumps the camp fuel into it. She stirs for a while, letting us get another pail ready, then puts it aside with a piece of wood over top of it. With the next pail ready, she repeats the process, and covers the second pail. The lid comes off the first and she stirs it again. I watch as she checks the consistency.

"What exactly are you looking for in that?" I ask.

"I want it to be thick, but not too much. It needs to be able to flow but also stick to stuff."

Jill shivers. "Stick to stuff?"

Mom nods. "Yes, the best war songs out of the sixties had lines like 'Napalm sticks to kids' and stuff like that." She takes one of the plastic bottles and starts scooping the mixture into it. "Good napalm should be almost like a jelly. This way we make it an oil-based and sticky product. The addition of the glycerine is a bonus."

Jill raises and eyebrow. "Why so?"

Mom smirks. "It'll wash those bikers away to hell."

"No, really?" Jill stops grating.

"Most of the napalm out there use plastics, like plates and such. The plastic is great for spreading but can go out if smothered and such. With the glycerine base, the fire will feed off the soap and blaze even under water. The soap creates bubbles, you see. The bubbles will then be able to feed the flame for it will be a pocket of air. No smothering. It also holds to what it is on like nothing else and doesn't get cold. It's like helping wash the Earth of the bikers for good."

"So, you said there's different types of napalm?" I ask.

"Yes, what we're making is going to be napalm M2. It will last longer than M4 and burns longer than M1. I'd rather make napalm-B but we don't have low-octane gas to burn. Rather leave what we got for Betsy, we'll need her when we do our good deed for the year and rescue those girls."

She has a plastic bottle full now and screws on the cap tight. "All we need is a fuse and something to light it with."

"You can use the power fuses you have for burning out stumps." I start to search in the back of the storage. "I know we used it a little over five years ago but it never goes bad in those packages."

"Then cut me off about a centimetre or so and let's go outside."

I find it, cut off a bit, and follow her outside. She's near the pond and is poking a small hole in the cap. I hand her the fuse and she stuffs it into the bottle.

"You have about three seconds on that one," I say, handing her the windless lighter.

"Good call on that, Steve." She flicks the lighter and it pushes out an invisible flame with a blue base. "Time to see what we got."

I don't know what I expected, but when she throws the lit bottle into the air. The fuse runs down and suddenly a fireball expands a good three metres round. Fire drops from the sky into the pond like rain. As it hits, the fire continues to burn. It lasts a good ten minutes. My mouth hangs open.

Mom grins. "Like I said, napalm sticks to kids."

13

PLAYING WITH FIRE

I lay awake for almost an hour. The darkness in the sky starts to give way to light, and Mindy is still sleeping. I don't want to wake her. Today is raid day. We've waited long enough to spring the biker's prisoners. Maybe that's not the right word for them, probably rape survivors is the correct term. Why would the women in the gang let the men do what they've done? Maybe they themselves are indoctrinated into the gang and only set free to be with one man after being broken. Really, I don't know. It's a bad situation in any case, but at least getting them out of the hands of their captors is all we can really do. Hopefully they're not brain washed.

Colette begs to come with us. She believes her husband is still alive. I don't think so, but if he is, we'll rescue him as well.

To make matters worse, the last of our good gas is just about done. Carl and Charlie hooked up some type of still and ran about two hundred litres of the stuff through it. Came out with only eighty litres of usable fuel, but it's clear of water and seems to be good. Charlie says that's the last time we'll be able to do that. The rest of the gas has been exposed to the elements for too long. It's not just the water, but the hydrocarbons or something that have broken down in it. The only way we can get something going is to raid one of the refinery plants in

Toronto, and I'm not going into that city with less than a tank and fighter jets to protect us.

Mindy stirs as the dull twilight in the sky brightens, allowing shadows to form and recede as the sun crawls toward the horizon. This is the magical time. She's asleep and lying on her side, the distended stomach holding our child is still there and right at this instance the world seems perfect, maybe even complete. The argument against me going on a raid has not been brought up and the rest of the world is peaceful, belying the havoc we're going to rain down on it.

A light scratching outside pulls at the strings of my memory, but it is probably a bird or something looking for nesting materials. It's early and they do that a lot in the summer. A little growl gets me out of bed quick, and Mindy moans at the disruption. I push open the window to get a good look beyond the dew-covered grass, searching for anything strange outside. There's not much to see, just a light fog on the lake and birds fluttering overhead. A cat meows softly and I think of Samantha. She's out there somewhere, probably just lazing about like she always did at home. I doubt she's hungry or starving. That cat could catch just about anything she put her mind to. Another meow, this time closer, draws my gaze to the side of the house. A tabby is on the roof of the kitchen staring up at me. Those little feet scramble and then it jumps to the window sill and to the other bedroom where Mom sleeps. The cat's nose sniffs at the air and she lets out a simple wanting cry before leaping. The distance is huge for a cat, but she makes it with just a few millimetres to spare. It walks to the window and rubs against the screen while letting out a soft purr.

"Samantha?" I can't believe it, my cat, my buddy, my baby. She found me.

I pull off the screen and Samantha walks through the window like it's nothing new to her. She jumps to the bed, sniffs Mindy, and licks her arm all the while purring intently. It seals the deal, this is Samantha. I've never seen any other cat lick people with such enthusiasm.

Mindy giggles, her arm reaching out and pulling the offending animal close to her. Sam lets out a little whine but goes along with it. There's stroking and kissing as Mindy says hello to my cat. Then her eyes open and go wide.

"Sammy?"

She lets go and Sam jumps off the bed and immediately comes over to me. I scoop her up in a shoulder-carry and she leans into me, rubbing the side of her face against mine. The purring becomes excessive.

"God, I've missed you, girl." I give her a squeeze and scratch between perked ears. Having her back lifts an unseen weight from my shoulders. She's one of the last missing pieces of my life. The day seems a little brighter now, air a bit crisper, and the outcome of today's mission a lot more hopeful. My family is together.

The plane sputters as Mom climbs up into the passenger's seat. Charlie and Carl worked on it for hours to get it leaned out enough for the ethanol rich fuel they dumped in it. They keep telling Danny it will run faster and hotter than before so not to push it too much. Maybe they should have gone back to the airport and taken the jet. No, that wouldn't work. They'd need some way to drop the bombs or using a plane would not be worthwhile, especially at the speeds the jet gets up to.

Carl hands up some of the improvised napalm jewels and Mom stuffs them all over the tight cubby hole. There's thirty of them, so I hope she knows what she's doing. The plan is we secure two diesel pickups at the Ford dealership in town as they start bombing the bikers. They need to take out what they can of our target's transportation and head north like before. Maybe the bikers will be confused and the ones who can ride will follow the plane. It's worked before.

Danny wanted to have wing mounted guns but both Carl and Charlie said no. Not enough time to build them and jury-rig a way to fire them from the cockpit. Mom has an AR just like Jill's so there's no concern. And they dumped a lot of clips into her pockets so I know she has enough ammo.

Carl demanded on coming with us but Jill and I both argued until he acquiesced. Mindy didn't demand on going, which was a relief. She did say when the pregnancy is over she and Jill will be having a long outback hunting trip while I look after our child. I only nodded and smiled. Easy enough to agree with that request, even though it would put her at risk.

We have four electric ATVs all charged up and ready to go. We're doubling up. Jill with me, Charlie and another guy, and two pairs on the other two. Wish I remembered their names. Too many people in the camp and not enough time to get to know them. If I know them and they get killed it'll hurt more, but at least they wouldn't be forgotten. Something about one of the couples makes my stomach churn, but that could be just my imagination.

"Remember to free as many women as you can. We'll buy you as much time as possible," Mom yells over the prop wash.

Danny increases the gas and the plane rolls forward, picking up speed. By the time it reaches the parking area she's got enough velocity to lift off. Over the tree tops they fly, up to about one thousand metres. No one is going to be able to shoot them from that height. The only problem is their bombs can only be dropped from about one hundred metres to be effective, less to have the desired effect. They'll figure it out.

I glance about the riders. "Ready?"

They all reply, even Jill who squeezes me and shouts in my ear. We all gun it and head for the dealership in Stouffville.

———

There's only a couple of corpses on the trip into town. We find three trucks in Stouffville, tanks half-filled but batteries dead. The ATVs come in handy that way. The batteries carry enough juice to boost the trucks and still get us around fast and quiet.

The engines complain and black smoke spills out the tail pipes but we're good to go. The trucks will last long according to Charlie, even though they'd been left out in the elements. The insides of the pistons are basically sealed off from rust forming and even if it did, it takes a lot to kill a diesel. Things are falling into place. We all take off back to Bloomington and ride toward Uxbridge.

Goodwood lies between Stouffville and Uxbridge. It's closer to

Stouffville, though. And as we get into the town, I slow down to take a good look at what has happened to my place. There's nothing left, just a few bricks and burnt sticks of logs poking out of the ground. All that hard work scrapping together money to buy it and poof, it's gone. Across the street, other homes have been burnt to the ground as well. I'm saddened by the loss and decide Pa got what was coming to him. We keep going on the road to town, leaving memories of another life behind.

It should only take us about ten minutes to get to Uxbridge. I check the charge on the ATV and it's still good. Lots of juice left for the run there and back.

We pass Concession four without any problem and follow forty-seven through the turn north, passing corpses on the side of the road in the ditches. They struggle to climb the sides as we head east again. The remnants of the chain link fence the bikers put up starts just before town and it looks a mess. Someone should have told them to keep it clean or the corpses would topple it over eventually. Bodies litter the road. Lots of skid marks show they rode through the area a few times maybe trying to clear the bodies.

The road turns northward, making us travel northeast as we enter town. The buzz of a plane overhead echoes and I watch something fall out of it. The small shape explodes into a firebomb about twenty feet off the ground and smoke rises from the town. Mom figured out the fuses and is making good use of our makeshift artillery.

Bikes run rough throughout the town and no one is paying attention to us. I don't mind that. The more they concentrate on the bombing the better our chances are of saving the women.

We pass Brock Street and hit Albert. Two turns finds us on Ash Street and heading toward the building the bikers have the women in. My rifle bangs against one shoulder and the bow the other. I don't go anywhere without my bow and two dozen arrows now. Almost bitten, twice shy.

Pa's old home passes by and we slow to pull up to Pine Ridge Apartments, a three story complex – the one the bikers use to house the women. Two bikers stand watch outside casually talking. The boredom of the duty hangs heavy on their shoulders. Jill leans out the window of the lead truck and fires off two rounds. Both men fall to the ground. She jumps out and runs over to them, kicks their guns aside and puts another round in each of their heads. No need to worry about them turning with holes through their brains.

The team makes its way to the front door on foot. One group will stay behind while the other three take care of each level. This way we're in and out. I'm on the top floor with Jill. We need to work fast.

If we come to a door we knock, letting the people know we're not going to hurt them. If it's locked, we use a crow bar to get in if they don't open it. Once we clear the rooms, we'll take the girls outside and put them on the trucks. That's the plan.

The first door isn't locked and we open it. I motion to Jill to announce us.

"Hello?" Jill calls out. "My name's Jill and I have a friend here, Steve. We're here to rescue you."

I motion to Jill and step into the room, rifle held ready but not pointed forward. A woman, maybe in her early twenties, cowers in the corner of a sectional couch. Her blonde hair is matted with sweat and grease, face battered and bruised. Makes me really like the bikers that much more. Wish I could give them all a present of a fast moving bullet. The girl is weeping, trying to hide herself under a blanket.

Jill slings her AR and approaches the girl. "It's okay, we're here for you."

"No," the girl whimpers. "No, I don't want to do anything. Don't hurt me."

Jill stops for a moment, hand stretched out ready to grasp the girl and pull her toward her. Not too long ago Mindy and I rescued Jill from a similar situation. I bet its running through her mind. The woman's eyes go wide and eyebrows arch up as Jill pushes back whatever she thought about.

"We're here to take you away from this place," she says, reaching out.

The girl cowers as her lower lip trembles. Her eyes well up with tears. "Don't kill me. I'll do it. Anything you want."

Jill cradles the woman in her arms. "Shush now, don't worry. No one's going to make you do anything you don't want to. Just come with us."

Hair is pushed aside and one swollen eye closes. Jill stands with the girl and her shirt hikes up enough to reveal massive bruising and welts. She's been beaten.

"Jill, we gotta keep moving," I whisper to her.

"Damn it, Steve. You should know what they're going to be like. It'll take the time it takes."

Jill walks the girl to the door. "We need to make sure everyone gets free." She turns back to the girl. "Is there anyone else on the floor with you?"

"Two others, I think." The girl is shuffling her feet, making the distance all that much greater.

A napalm bomb goes off on the other side of the street followed by the buzzing of a plane passing overhead. The girl crouches. This is something she probably hasn't heard for a long time.

"That… is that you?" she asks.

"My mom is in that plane buying us time, but it's not going to last," I say. "Let's get going."

We head to the next door and bang on it. A gun fires from inside. I duck aside as the metal door rings.

"Fuck you!" a man's voice comes from the other side. "You want some of me? You can have it! I'm done with the girl, and I'm going to fuck you hard and put bullets into your ass." Another shot files. "You'll shit my cum for a week!"

The door's unlocked.

I sense a theme here.

I give it a quick shove and it opens, striking the biker behind it. He staggers back. I put a bullet into his chest. No time to fool around, just get in and out.

The layout of the place is the exact opposite of the other, and I end up heading into the bedroom as opposed to the front room. It's the right type of accident for all the wrong reasons. The girl is dead. Bullet to the brain. Bruises adorn her pretty face and one lip is split, blood still caked on it. That's what the biker did before coming to the door.

Ligature marks encircle her wrists along with cigarette burns up her arms.

I head to the door just as Jill is peaking in. "The girl?"

What else can I do? I shake my head. "Biker got her."

Our guide takes us to another room own the other hall. There's a girl looking out the door, no more than eleven. She's just a kid. Our woman runs to the kid and embraces her. The little one starts to cry. We collect them, direct our steps to the stairs and outside. One of the other crew fared better than us, they have six while we wait for the last crew to come out from the second floor.

About a minute of anxiety passes. Shots ring out. Girls scream and a man's voice joins them. Jill and I rush for the door to help. Charlie is there with his helper for the day. Our man is staring at a big guy blocking most of the hallway with his shoulders. To say he is big would be like saying the leaning tower of Pizza has a slight tilt. I pull out my Glock and slam the butt against the biker's head. He goes down. The guy he's holding goes down. Three women scream and rush out in various levels of undress. I pull the biker off our man and help him up.

"Thanks for the assist," he rasps out while gulping breath.

"Don't mention it," I say. "Let's get the girls and get out of here."

Another explosion rocks the air. This one is close.

"Davis and across. Hurry!"

We get all the girls into the trucks and speed off toward Concession seven. From there we run up onto Davis Drive and across. The plane makes one more pass over Uxbridge and heads north in almost the same direction. No one should be watching us. None of them will know what happened until they decide it's time to rape someone. None of them will be happy. It will be too late for them to do anything but curse us for making off with what they consider their property. It's a win. We've beaten them again and this time we probably killed a lot of their bikes. They won't be bothering us for an awful long time – if we did everything right.

I have two girls in the truck with me, the ones Jill and I rescued. Easier that way. They're probably still scared witless of men after the bikers, but putting them with someone else would traumatize them even more.

"You're okay now. We'll take you to the camp we have set up and get you some help." I swerve to get around a wrecked car. "Then you can get a good meal and a decent night's sleep in a warm bed."

My Glock is pulled out of its holster and the woman points it at me.

"Now hold on," I say. "We're rescuing you from them."

"I'm not going to go through that again," she says through tears. "No one is going to have me like that."

"Of course not, we're saving you from them."

"I'm not going to be your slave." She slips off the safety. "Never again." Steady streams of tears fall all over her and the young girl sitting on her lap. "Neither of us will."

"That's right, neither of you will have to put up with anything like that again," I say, slowing the truck down. "We're taking you to a sa–"

"You're taking us nowhere." She places the gun against the child's temple and pulls the trigger.

Blood fills the cabin. The echo of the shot rings in my ears. I swerve to the side and then back again. Tires scream as we straighten out on the road. I reach out to grab at the gun but she's right against the door, muzzle pressed to her temple. A second passes as her eyes lock on mine. Her lips form the words that will stick in my mind forever. *I don't believe you.* She pulls the trigger and the cabin of the truck is filled with blood and gun smoke once again. The noise of the Glock hammers my ears once more. I see half of her head open to the air, the rest of it is plastered against the back of the truck.

14

GROUND WORK

We scattered after freeing the women from captivity. I couldn't even pull over to take another truck. Each person took one vehicle, it just so happened Jill and I grabbed trucks. Strange how it worked out, but since the rescued women would be more comfortable with those who rescued them or other women, the decision happened well before the raid. Two women sit beside me. Their lives snuffed out without even a chance at being free again. A waste. There are so few of us now.

I stare out at the world around us. It's a mess, and I don't know how to help fix it any more. My knuckles turn white as I grip hard. A scream of frustration erupts from my mouth. One of my hands hammer the steering wheel. Hatred wells up inside and my stomach burns.

"I'm sorry." It's empty words, and does nothing to close the eyes of the women in the seat next to me. I'm not going to dump their bodies on the road. They deserve better than that.

My route back to camp is the usual I took as a kid returning from Uxbridge, up to Davis and across to Ninth. Direct, and easy. There are few vehicles on the road and none are blocking it. The plane's engine drones above me. It sputters as the last of the good gas burns in the pistons. They'll have to really work on it to get it to run on the ethanol fuel. I surmise Danny's flying low to make sure they don't crash or something if the fuel actually stalls the engine out.

A quick crank lowers the window; a little and fresh air starts to replace the scent of death. Fuck, why did she have to go and do that? We saved her from hell and she thought we were taking her to another one. But we weren't. If only she could have seen it. Why was my Glock easy to get at? I'll never know the answers to those questions, but they keep rolling through my head.

The turn for Ninth Line comes into view and I start to slow. No need to make a big show out of what I'm doing. Danny banks the plane south as well, dipping down to just above treetop level. I don't like the sound of the engine. It keeps going from strong to cough and back again. At least we're close to home.

I admit, the trucks are performing well. When Charlie and Carl mentioned using diesel I thought they were insane, but they fired up when powered and have worked well since. There's little noise from the engine and it rides smoothly. Guess we'll need to get a bunch more of them soon. Carl said the fuel will last for a few years as long as we can find it. Doesn't break down like gasoline. Just have to filter out the sludge. At least we have good news, even if I'm transporting dead bodies to the camp. We can give them a decent burial when we lay them to rest.

St. John's Sideroad rushes by and the plane sounds as if it's limping through the sky. The flight isn't stable, but up and down, left and right. Something is wrong. The engine sputters even more than before, like trying to pull in gas and failing.

"We're almost home, don't quite on us now."

Danny told me the stall speed of the bi-plane is sixty. Its top speed only a hundred and fifty. I pace it and glance at my speedo, she's only at seventy. Good for approach but not good when you have almost two kilometres to run. The plane banks off a little and straightens. She's lining up for her landing.

Aurora Road comes up and I slow just in case someone else is running in from another direction. Just as expected, another truck rolls to the intersection filled with women. Must be Jill. She waves me through. Good thing, didn't want to have to stop behind her with the two bodies in the truck. Won't help those in hers.

The plane dips behind the tree tops. Must be going in to land now. I drive through the intersection and turn onto the bush trail where the power lines are. Jill will take the regular road hopefully. This will give me time to stash this truck and clean it out later. I want the bodies out before things get too gruesome.

It's not the nicest ride into camp, but there'll be less people here. Most will be at the road block on the driveway taking care of it. I power over a ditch, run up onto the small road in the camp, and head to the house. The truck handles the ground well as I aim for the small fire pit behind the building. The bodies can go into the bush and we'll be a lot safer for it. I can clean up at the house from the old hand pump. Lake water won't hurt me.

A memory of swimming in the large pond comes to mind. Small fish scattering and little feet pounding into the water from shore. I snap back to reality, a pair of dead eyes staring at nowhere remind me of our broken world.

There are people still in camp, not many. Some wave while a few others stare. They must see the bodies against the door or wonder what I'm doing. Hopefully they'll keep their distance while I remove the bodies. Such a waste of life.

I get to the small clearing, stop, and pull out the bodies. The two jostle to the ground with little effort. It's messy work with the wounds. My shirt is covered in slow cooling blood and my pants are brownish red between the belt and knees.

"What happened?" a voice echoes from the top of the clearing.

I spin, reflexively reach for my Glock, but relax as I recognize her voice. The world spins. My knees buckle a little and I drop to them. Both hands come up and cover my face. Grief floods through me.

"I couldn't stop them." The sound is a hundred miles away.

Mindy runs to me, bends down, catches my body as I start to fall. She's going to ruin her clothes. One of her hands starts to stroke my blood matted hair.

"We got them out. These two, but on the ride back…" The image plays through my mind. I'm there again, watching it happen, trying to get her to stop. "She grabbed my gun, shot the little one and then herself. Didn't want to be a slave any longer."

She rocks me back and forth, hand still stroking my head.

"I tried to tell her we were saving them. They're not slaves anymore, but she put the muzzle to the little girl's temple and pulled the trigger before I could get anything out." The gun shot echoes through my mind. "She turned it on herself and... Oh, Mindy." The second shot echoes louder than the first.

There's another shot. These are not in my mind. I have to pull myself together. Bury the feelings of guilt for not bringing them home. Find out what's happening. The two girls are dead. I tried to protect them but failed. Now, there's something wrong at camp. I'm not going to fail them. Too many people need me, rely on me, look to me for assistance.

I untangle from Mindy and push myself to my feet. One arm comes up and wipes away the dribble from my face. No time to be crying when work needs to be done. I glance to Mindy, her eyes shining with moisture. "Stay here, be safe. Protect our child." With that, I walk to the truck and pull out my rifle. She's right behind me. I turn to her. "Here, in case you need it."

"What about you?" Mindy asks.

Her beautiful eyes stare at me. "I need to find out what's happening up there."

"Be careful," Mindy says, but it doesn't register as I jump into the truck and drive away.

I round the house. Someone is shooting and I don't know where it's coming from. Jill's truck is parked outside in the playground area and the girls are all hunkered down on this side of it. That tells me the shots are coming from the opposite direction. I head to Jill's truck. Get the thing pulled to the left of the tailgate, and slide over to the passenger door to exit. The girls from Jill's truck are huddled against the tire. The smaller one's lip trembles. Nonsense comes out of her while tears stream down one cheek. The others hold on to one another, heads bent down and together. Another shot rings out.

I pop open the door and slide out. A bullet hits the driver's door window, sending small shards everywhere. I duck down to keep from getting splattered by the small projectiles. A quick crawl and I'm beside Jill. She's nursing her arm.

"What the hell happened?" I glance around and count the people. None are dead.

"Lucky shot. Just a graze, though." She lifts her arm and shows me the shot. There's blood, but not much. "What the hell happened to you?"

I glance over at the other women. "I'll tell you later."

She nods slightly, as if to tell me she'll remember this talk. "One of the girls must have been a plant or something. They got in here and started shooting at us. The girls were out of my truck but that didn't stop one from getting hit as well."

I can't get a good look around. "All the trucks here?"

"Yes, but they took out one."

"Shit." I get my feet under me in a crouch. A quick glance over the box shows the other truck at the top of the drive. The flash of a rifle firing warns me, and I duck just as the round flies overhead. "Crap, they're keeping a good eye on us." I slump back down. "Where's your AR?"

"In the truck. Tried to get it but they shot when the door opened."

The muzzle of the rifle sticks up through the passenger window. Should be easy to get, but then again, this was supposed to be an easy raid. I crawl over to the passenger door, motion for the women to give me a little room. Just a quick pop up and snatch, that's all that's needed. I start to stand. Make sure my body is by the cab support post. Almost there, just a little more. I reach out and yank the AR out of the cab. Bullets pop through the driver door and a window explodes sending a shower of small pieces to the ground. I slump back down and crawl to Jill with a smile on my face.

"Whatcha going to do with that?" she asks.

"Watch," I say, laying down into a prone position.

The sight is good, but not that powerful. In all the gun fights where people use vehicles to hide behind, none use the obvious tactic of shooting under and taking out legs. I line up the sight, put the bead on a leg. They're making the basic mistake of not moving every once in a while. The vehicle is safe. It protects you from everything. That's the mindset. I breathe in, centre the target, hold, the trigger slowly depresses. The suppressed bark of the AR is nothing compared to the other weapons.

The NATO .556 round has a good punch and it smashes through the leg bone. The woman drops, screaming in pain.

I keep scanning the truck. "Is she the only one?"

"Don't think so. Too many rounds being fired for it to be just one shooter."

A shot hits the side of the truck.

"Where's the other shooter?"

"I think she's behind one of the tires."

"Smart." I shift my aim. A few shots in one of the rear tires will cause someone to shift and that's when I'll have them.

Jill's gun rings out beside me. Fuck, I'm going to be deaf soon if this keeps up. I swing the scope over and the one I shot is now dead, her rifle pointed at us. Should have known.

The restricted AR is the closest we can get to auto. You have to keep squeezing the trigger for it to work well. I take aim at the rear tire. I think that's where the person will be, away from the other to cover a better cross fire. Three quick shots cause the tire to just about explode. The resulting pop and release of air forces the person step out from behind it, their legs in the clear. I pull off a couple of rounds and the breach locks open. Out of ammo.

"Another clip!" I call back.

"They're in the truck."

"Time to bluff." I crawl back and get onto my feet, hunched over to not give a target. "You're out numbered," I yell. "There's others in the woods coming in to surround you. Time to give yourself up."

I don't know what to expect, but the voice that drifts over is not it. "No fucking way."

It's a woman's voice. Deep but not too much. I can tell she smokes, or smoked. Must be a bit older. Fuck, she must be the one who watched over the women. How'd we miss her?

"I can promise that no harm will come to you if you give up now." I glance at Jill. She shrugs.

"Yeah, I heard what you did at the Wallymart last year to the guys," the woman yells over. "Killed a bunch of them for just wantin' what's theirs."

I try to remember how many rounds she's fired. "How many clips you think she has?"

"Not sure, maybe three or four?"

Five to ten rounds in a clip, three or four clips. Thirty to forty rounds. If she's been firing as support then that would put her between twenty and thirty rounds fired. Another shot rings out. She's fired over twenty.

"I know you're Steve, so I'm going to git into the truck and drive away from here. I'll shoot anyone who gets in my way."

Not much to say about it. The woman wants to retreat. Probably saw everyone at the road and decided the best thing to do was run.

"The truck's ours, you're not taking it anywhere," I call out. "Besides, it's probably low on fuel and nowhere around here to fill it up." That should get her. Get her to think we've used up all the resources.

Air is still. I wait for another shot or yell back. Agonizing seconds pass as we wait.

"Steve!" Carl bellows. "I got her."

Jill and I stand from behind the truck. Carl is there, his gun trained on the woman, her rifle over his shoulder. She has her hands up in surrender. He must have snuck around while we talked. That's why he's my best friend.

I walk around the truck and head over to him. Jill follows behind me, Glock hanging loose in her grip.

"Got around from the gate and snuck up from behind the big tree there." He motions to the spruce at the parking lot by the playground. "Once I got behind her she gave up. Knew what was going wrong in her plan. A guy with a gun."

"Good job, man." I come up, raise my rifle, and covering the still-open breach. "You can relax now."

Carl lowers his arms, comes over, and I take his Gock, handing him the empty rifle. He stares at it.

The woman tries to kill me with her gaze. "You were empty?"

Jill raises my Glock. "I wasn't."

"Frisk her, will you Jill?" I put the gun into my right hand. "Don't miss anything. I want to make sure there's nothing she can do to us."

Jill pushes the woman against the truck. The plant puts her hands on it in order not to smash her face. A kick between the feet drives the woman to stand, spread and subject herself to a search. Jill doesn't miss anything. Two knives, pack of Players Special Blend, wooden matches, flask, and a small Dillinger. The small two shot gun is just easy enough to hide if someone wasn't being especially careful searching. It's so nice I decide to give it to Mindy as a present. She'll love it.

With a yank, Jill turns the woman around to face her. Both hands pat down the woman's front where she finds bobby pins and a the padded bra. Her hands go inside it, finding another knife and garrote. Looks like she wanted to be sure of escape if needed.

"So, whatcha going to do to me beside make me hot, Jill," the woman says.

Carl motions with a hand at the woman. "You know her?"

"Yeah, she's one of Pa's right hands, or was." Jill takes off the woman's watch. "Thought it was her, but she's a lot uglier now than a few years ago."

The woman spits at Jill, hitting her in the cheek. Jill just wipes it off.

"Wow, and here we thought of just getting a couple of women free from the bikers." Jill smiles.

"They're comin, ya know." The woman glares at Jill. "I'll take ya as my slave girl. Make you walk around with cut out panties and no bra for the rest of your life, which won't be long."

Jill backhands the woman, making her head bounce back. There's a smile on the woman's face as she spits out blood.

"I'm going to enjoy stuffing things up your ass."

Carl steps forward, grabbing Jill's arm before she can hit the woman again. "Enough, babe. She's trying to goad you into either killing her or making a mistake."

"My mistake was not killing her when I saw her." Jill pulls her hand away. "We have tape or something?"

"I'll get it." With a glance at the woman, I take off to the shed.

It's only sixty meters away but that's far enough not to hear what's going on. In the tool shed I hunt for what she wants and come up with duct tape. Good enough for just about anything. When I step out, the women from Jill's truck are gathered around the other truck and they're all talking with Jill, explaining what happened to them under the rule of this woman. My gut heaves threatening to spew as I approach. Seems the woman liked using a strap on and anal. I block out a lot of it. They get to how she likes them young, maybe around ten or so, and my stomach flips. The kid. That young thing we saved on the top floor was only maybe ten. That means this woman probably put her through hell and back again for her own pleasure – a child molester to boot.

I hand the tape to Jill who puts a strip across the woman's mouth. She binds the woman's hands making sure she doesn't keep her elbows together. She then tapes the elbows together and smiles. "Not getting out of that one, Gretchen."

First time I hear her name. Eastern European but no accent. At least second generation.

The women argue about what to do to Gretchen. Some want to outright kill her, others want to let her go, hoping the sign of good faith will go a long way. The rest of the camp starts to come together including Danny and Mom. Mindy is close behind. She gives me a knowing look, blood all over her hands. Collette comes out with Zoey but backs up a little when she sees Gretchen bound up. Smart woman. She corrals Zoey and they disappear into the house. Wish we found her husband on the raid, but not much you can do with explosions ringing out around you.

Mom comes over and tears the tape off Gretchen's mouth. "We want information."

Gretchen goes to spit at her but Mom uppercuts her so fast that she bites her tongue. Blood seeps from the corners of her mouth. "Ya can't make me talk, bitch."

"I'm a CSIS trained interrogator, I've made people stronger than you talk, fucker. How much do you like water?"

15

WICKED SMILE

People go white, or pale, for a number of reasons. It could be blood loss, the cold, getting sick, or the thought of someone torturing you. But Gretchen is made of stronger stuff than that. She just gives a smile and a toss of her head.

The afternoon sun warms up the area nicely, but something cold eeks inside my bones. It could be just about anything. Maybe it's the icy hard look Mom levels at the woman.

"I'll give ya nothing," Gretchen says.

"Fine, you either give us what we need voluntarily or I'll get it out of you the old fashion way." Mom looks at me. "Got a pen and paper?"

I stare at her with blank eyes. "No, you want me to get one?"

Mom shakes her head. "Yes, you'll find one in the storage shed."

I take off at a good jog. The paper and pen are inside the shed where they're always hanging. A quick grab and I jog back to the group. Mom's explaining how things are going to proceed.

"...about torture is there's no real way to verify the information unless you screw up." She takes the pen and paper from me. "Some of the people I trained never thought much about doing stupid things and that usually led to the person they were interrogating dying. I'm not like that. You see, if I get information from you the first thing I'm going to do is verify it before letting you go." She scribbles something on the pad. "And when it turns out to be wrong, you'll have to deal with the consequences. It's easy to lie, but it's hard to back things up with the truth. You don't know how much I know, or if I'm asking you a question to verify you're telling the truth or I just don't know that answer." She rips off the page and hands it to me. "Steve, love. Do your mother a favour and get those things from for me."

I glance at the list. Salt, pepper, chili flakes, vinegar, sand, paper towel. It doesn't make sense. When I look up to ask a question she has no expression on her face, just a flaccid expression showing no emotion. Even her voice is flat. "Now, please."

With a simple nod I take off to the house. Almost all the list is in the kitchen so I pick it up and put it into small sack to carry. Sand. Not sure what she wants with that, but I'll get it. There's also a few other things like needle and thread. What a strange mixture of items.

As I'm searching for the needle and thread, Colette comes down the stairs and gives me a side long glance. "What you looking for?"

"Needle and thread." And before she can ask another question, I say, "Don't ask."

She holds up her hands. "Wasn't going to. Try the other drawer, I think there's some in there."

Sure enough, there they are. I put them in the sack. "Just need some sand now."

"Beach by the lake. Take a cup or something so you can scoop water into it as well. Not sure what you're doing but it sounds interesting now. Want company?"

Yeah, that'd be fun. Sounds like a date at the movies. Watch someone get tortured. Not sure she would like that, knowing how she gets. "Not this time. Keep Zoey inside will you?"

"Sure, but I want to know what happens."

"Only if you haven't eaten before I tell you."

I leave the house and head to the lake. Everyone is around the shed now, moving things out under Mom's guidance. Really want to know what they're doing, but I guess I'll find out soon enough. I scoop sand into a cup and add water. Not a lot, just enough to keep it wet.

As I walk toward the shed, the air gets heavy. The people are moving about and doing what Mom tells them, but a hesitation in the way they're doing it that tells me they're unsure. They constantly glance back to clarify instructions. Maybe they're losing their nerve about doing this and don't really want to know how the biker gang operates. I've seen it first hand on me, been on the receiving end just like the women we rescued. Nothing is going to stop me from putting an end to them. If this is the reboot of the world then I want to make sure the good people survive.

Two tables are set up, one with an end raised a lot, giving it a good incline. Not sure what that's for, but it won't be good. I dump the requested items onto the empty table. Mom left the soap, kerosene and a few other items in plain sight but I don't think she's told Gretchen what I was to get. Three chairs are at one end of the shed, two of them facing one. Gretchen sits in the lone one, taped down tight.

Mom looks at the people who assisted her. "Okay, thanks for helping with that. Now get going, you don't want to be around for this."

Doc steps forward. "You'll need me here in case something happens."

"If anything happens, Doc, I'll take care of it. You don't need or want to see this." She gives him a gentle shove.

"If Steve is staying then I'll stay as well," Jill says. "I've been through what they do with people and I can tell you if what you're doing is going to work or not."

"No, you won't," Mom says. "I've done this many times and you have no idea what I can do, and you'll just be a distraction."

She leans in a little close and whispers something. Jill goes pale. That ends it right there. I'm not sure I want to be there.

"You just can't torture someone. Let them tell you what they know first," someone shouts. A couple of people join in but they soon quiet down as they look over to see the women we rescued. The mass of them stand together, hair in tangles, dirty, unwashed for what appears weeks. All sport bruises on their bodies if not their faces. Several have cigarette burns on their arms.

Mom turns to the crowd. "You all know who I am, and what lengths I'll go to protect the group. This is no different than." She takes a deep breathe. "You came here for protection and safety. I'm supplying it. Now we have an issue of others in danger, and I'm going to bring them into our fold for the same protection you enjoy as well."

"We need to remain civilized, or there's no reason to keep going," Cindy says.

Mom glares at her. "And that is the problem." She runs a hand through her short hair. "All those wars our country fought before this happened were wrong."

"We agree, war is wrong," a middle aged may says. I think his name is John.

"No, we fought them wrong," Mom states. "Remember the first and second World Wars? They had the same theme throughout, win by killing masses. If you don't take them out from the ground up, the fighting will take forever to finish. Civilians tell the government how long to fight, and if you start killing them, the pressure to end the war comes from the people to those who plan the fight."

Mom shakes her head. "But this is not a democracy. If you don't like the protection that is offered here, you can leave. I'm going to do what is needed to ensure we survive."

The group mumbles for a few seconds but none step forward to challenge her. Mom can be very domineering when she wants to. And with that, she nods to me and walks into the shed.

I follow her and close the door, leaving the group to do what they want. Gretchen stares at us, eyes level and unblinking, chin somewhat thrust out. I doubt anything will get through to her. But Mom sits down in front of her and smiles. I can almost see ice form around her and that scares the hell out of me. This woman has the ability to take the current situation and play it against any person she wants. Nothing will take her away from what it is she seeks from the other person. The truth.

The pen and paper sits on the table and she picks it up.

"I only have a few questions. Depending on what your answers are will determine how uncomfortable or painful this will be. Understand?"

Gretchen's brow furrows, eyes darting from Mom to me.

"Well, I'll take that as a yes." She poises the pen and starts her questioning. "How many of you are still alive? Where are you getting your gas? What have you done with the others you have taken? These are the simple questions I want you to answer, nothing more, nothing less." She reaches over and takes hold of the tape edge. "I'm taking this off and I want the answers." She pulls it back slowly.

Gretchen spits at Mom. "Fuck you."

Mom puts the tape back. "Not smart." She reaches over to the table and grabs the box of salt. "So, we'll start simple and work our way up to the hard stuff." She displays the salt for Gretchen to see, opens it, and pours a little bit out. "This will not be nice, but you'll recover from it easily. Out of all I'm going to do, this one will not have any lasting damage. Steve, get me a jug of water, just in case."

There's still some of the bottled water from the bomb building we did so I grab one and twist off the top. I don't know what to do so just stand there and wait for the show. It doesn't take long before I realize the salt is going somewhere I may not want to watch.

You can do a lot to a person in order to make them talk, but unless it's something that will really hurt or damage, most can shake it off. I would think the most sensitive places would be the best to start, but then again, I'm just a computer geek.

Mom stands and walks around to the back of Gretchen's chair. She grabs a handful of hair and pulls back. Salt pours out of Mom's hand and into the woman's nostrils. Not a lot from what I can see. The woman struggles not to breathe, but with her mouth covered, she has no choice but to do so through her nose, and thus through the salt pouring into it.

"Once you're ready, I'll stop."

Mom pours a little more salt into Gretchen's nose. The struggling intensifies. She tries to jerk against the bonds and clear her nose. Phlegm bubbles, making a gurgling sound as air passes it. The sound becomes harsher and her face reddens. Mom holds out her hand for the water and I put the bottle into it. She pours it right into her nose, let's go of the hair, and rips off the tape over her mouth.

Gretchen's head falls forward as she gasps and spits up water. Tears fill her eyes. She gasps and spittle splatters from her mouth. "Fuck you!"

"Well, if you're at that already this shouldn't take too long," Mom says. She puts down the water and picks up the pad and pen again. "How many of you are still alive? Where are you getting your gas? What have you done with the others you have taken?"

Gretchen raises her head part way. An air of defiance makes its way from her eyes, through strands of wet hair, and hits Mom. "Fuck off."

"Maybe the number of questions are confusing you. How many of you are still alive?"

"Eat shit."

Mom glances around and finds the duct tape. She pulls off a strip and puts it over Gretchen's mouth. One hand goes into the bag and pulls out the black pepper. "This usually works. I've had very little hold up to this and still not break. It's not nice, so you better be ready for it." Mom rips off a strip of duct tape and double seals Gretchen's mouth. Once again, she walks to the back of the chair and pulls Gretchen's hair, tilting her head back at what I understate as uncomfortable. Pepper goes into the nose. Not a lot, just a steady amount to make sure the woman breathes it in against her will. Water streams from the corners of wide eyes. Chest convulses. Urine wafts in the air. A face turns red.

There's no call for water, just a waiting game to see how much pain the woman will endure before breaking. Gretchen holds up well. Even with her struggling for air there's still defiance in her eyes. Desire to not give anything. But the sneezing with a gag is disturbing.

The tape is ripped off and hair let go. No water. Gretchen sputters, coughs, and sneezes. She tries to take in a breath but her body convulses just enough to make it difficult. Phlegm with black pepper spatters on the floor. She convulses again, sneezing with little air getting into her lungs. Bowels release gas. I wait for the questions to start once more, but Mom appears to have another thing in mind. She grabs the salt, pulls back a fist full of hair again, and pours some on closed eyes. Before Gretchen can shake it off, Mom puts her thumbs on the eyes and starts to grind. Not hard, just enough to get the salt past the lids. Gretchen tries to throw her head from side to side, so Mom pries open a bottom lid and throws more salt into an eye. She holds the lid open, not letting Gretchen blink. Tears stream and a body struggling to breathe jerks spasmodically. Mom lets go and steps back.

There is no fluctuation in the voice that comes out of Mom. No emotion. Cold and level. "How many of you are still alive?"

Gretchen lifts her head, nose running, tears streaming down her face, one eye swollen almost completely shut. For a second, I see something in her. It could be anything, but it's not defiance this time. She is breaking from the pain, but I don't think she's there yet.

"No comment? Not going to insult me?" Mom sighs. "Thought you were made of tougher stuff."

Redness climbs up Gretchen's face and she grits uneven teeth, lips pulling back. Her voice rasps, "I'm… I'm not telling you anything."

Mom smiles. "There's the defiant attitude I expect. Guess that's why they have you as second in command of The Family."

There's a crack in the armour around the woman. A hesitation concerning a comeback. "You don't know what you're talking about."

Mom smirks. "The one thing about people is when they're in a stressful situation, their body language tells a lot." She leans into her. "Think what else can be done to you." Mom stands, and steps to the back of the captive. She reaches out to the table, grabs the sand in water, and quietly removes the lid.

Again, Mom takes a handful of hair and pulls back, angling the other eye upward. She dumps the wet sand onto the lids and forces them open, putting as much under the bottom lid as possible. Gretchen screams. Bile threatens to climb up my throat.

Mom leans into the woman and whispers something in her ear. There's trembling, then water washes out the sand. It takes a bit, and Mom is meticulous with how she does the cleaning. Gretchen let's her know how much it hurts with little outbursts.

Once finished, Mom sits down in front of the other woman and asks, "How many of you are still alive?"

"Just over two hundred," Gretchen whimpers.

"Where are you getting your gas?"

"We… we've been raiding the stations all over." Gretchen's head bobs a little as she stares at her knees. "There's captives in the Southerland pit."

We let Doc into the shed with a promise he'll not undue her bindings. Only a few of the people stayed to see what happened to Gretchen. They give us a wide birth as we walk past them.

"You hungry?" Mom's voice comes out as if we just came back from a long walk.

"Little." I don't understand how. My stomach is still a bit knotted up but slowly unravelling.

"Good, strong stomach is a good thing to have."

We walk to the house. About half way there, Mom takes my hand. "She's lying, you know."

"About what?"

"How many they have left." Mom squeezes my hand. "They have a lot less than two hundred. I'd be surprised if they have one hundred."

I'm shocked. She had me convinced. "What makes you think she's lying about how many they have?"

"You just have to count," Mom says. "They'd have more girls. Bikers like sex. They're dominant A-typical. And they don't like to share." She lets out a breath. "You didn't find any boys being molested?"

"No, not there."

"Northern group. Probably homophobic."

"And the gas?"

"Makes sense. It was my test question, let me know if she was lying or not." Mom let's go of my hand. "They've only done exactly what we've done, maybe a little less effective."

Weighing the statement makes sense. The answers to the questions came out certain ways without telling me anything, but Mom has a way about her to find out what she wants. I could never get a lie past her regardless of how I tried.

"So, what makes you think the last part is true?"

"The answer was perfect, just like the gas."

The truck is something I'll never get used to. Diesels are supposed to be loud and smelly, this thing is quiet and anything but. Charlie should be out soon, said he had to go to the bathroom before we took off to the Southerland pit for a rescue. Carl wanted to go, but the Doc still demands a couple more days of rest for him. I would have made fun of it, but I know all too well what Doc's like. And he still doesn't like that I'm going, but all I have is a head wound and stitches, no bullet holes in my back. At least not any more.

I switch the radio on for the hell of it and spin it over to where there should be music. Nothing but static. Even the local station from Stouffville is quiet, but that's not a surprise. I switch to satellite and let the thing scan, watching the channels tick away like the time on a digital clock.

The door opens and Colette jumps in the cab. She wasn't picked to come. Charlie should be back soon. This is all wrong.

"Charlie's coming with me today." It sounds weak even to me when I say it.

"Yeah? Well, so am I." She crosses her arms, stares out the front windshield.

"I don't think you understand, Charlie—"

"No, you don't understand," Colette says. "Peter's out there and I'm going to get him with or without you."

She's headstrong, just like Mindy. Only a few weeks ago she would have cowered at the thought of imposing her will on someone. Now, with all that's gone on, she's the boss of all of us. "Okay, do you have a weapon?"

She stares out the window. "Don't need one."

"What if we run into trouble?"

"You'll kill it."

Can't argue with her there. Either Charlie or I will take care of it. "Still, you need something." I open the arm rest and pull out my spare Glock, check the safety, and ensure the clip is full. "Know how to use this?"

"Aim down the barrel and squeeze. Bullet goes into the bad guys."

"Funny. Okay, Charlie is just going to be a minute or so. You want shotgun?"

Her nod is slight, but I catch it. "Okay, well, you'll be responsible for making sure I don't get lost along the way, and keeping us safe on the road."

"I can do that."

Charlie knocks on the window. Colette lowers it.

"Didn't think you were coming," Charlie says.

"Wouldn't miss it for the world," Collette says, turning to me with a wicked smile. "Can we go now?"

16

SNATCH AND GRAB

About twenty minutes, that's how long the drive to the Sandford pit would usually be, but it's taking us longer than I imaged. Between weaving around cars and corpses from the tail end of the herd it's going to take twice as long. And, being the one watching the road in order to get us there is the hard part.

I don't think Colette likes Charlie. They don't speak once he's in the car and neither of them are talking to me besides the "watch out for that corpse!" sort of thing. Hell, might as well of brought the cat, at least she'd sit on my lap and purr.

We get a few kilometres outside of the small village of Sandford when the radio comes to life. The satellite scan finds something. There's no static, only dead air and then sound. It's not much, almost like a whispering, as if someone has left a phone off the hook, but it's someone. We all lean forward. It's been a long time since we've heard anything else but the sound of our own voices and the noise of someone else is somewhat disturbing. Then it happens. Music. Almost canned at first, but soon it clears up and definitely an acoustic guitar and some woman singing. It's not English, something like French. We're all sitting there with our mouths hanging open.

Colette turns up the volume a little. "Anyone know what language that is?"

Charlie shakes his head. "No, like French but not exactly."

"Has a Slavic feel to it, don't you think?" Colette looks at me.

"Don't look at me. Can someone jot down the station and satellite so we can come back to it in camp?"

"Got it," Charlie says.

"I'm going to make it scan more, just in case." I set it to roll again, run through the channels. Nothing.

By the time we're at the pits, the station is back on and we're listening to the same song. I stop, motion for the other two trucks to pull up.

"We got a signal on the radio. Station five two seven on satellite four. Anyone heard this language before?"

Jill turns her radio on first but shakes her head.

In the other truck, one of the older guys scratches his head and looks a little puzzled with drawn brow. "I think it's Chippawas. Almost sounds like their language."

"Well, whatever it is, I think we need to investigate, but after we get the people out of here." There's a gate across the front, locked and uninviting. "Who's going to ram?" I ask.

Jill steps on the gas and the short gate parts as she hits it, the chain ripping its way through the links. She's leading the pack now, so I keep up.

It was easier with the plane, but we have no fuel for it. Hopefully it won't take long to distil something to burn in it. But like Carl and Charlie said, we have to replace the lines or they'll deteriorate faster than we can shake a stick at a corpse. Won't do much good to have the plane fly for a while only to be grounded for longer while we replace the rubber with plastic tubes.

The gravel road forks. A house stands on the right side and the pit on the left. It's a deep one, probably years old. Wonder if they hit bedrock. Like all the others the bikers have used, this one has a steep ramp going down and a raised island in the middle. The gully is filled with corpses mulling about looking for anything to eat. They're trapped just like the others. This one will not be an easy rescue. Even with a lot of help, the people may need to sit in the flat beds, leaving them exposed. The corpses may find a way at them in their unprotected escape. Sometimes I wish the van had survived.

Colette starts to cry. Her tough exterior melts away like snow on a hot spring day. She's returning the young woman she really is. A few seconds pass and she's blabbering.

I stop the truck and throw it into park. "What's wrong?"

"Peter… he's dead."

I don't understand what she's talking about. We've been operating on the assumption he was still alive. "Don't say that, he's still alive. We'll find him."

"He's dead." Her lower lip trembles. "I see him there." Colette points into the pit.

I don't see it, not now. Then, one of the corpses turns and the face, or what's left of it, is Peter's. He's in the pit at the edge. His lumbering form keeps pace with the other corpses as they promenade around the excavation on their endless hunt for flesh. Milky eyes focus on nothing.

Colette's worse fear is devastating. She stares at what was once her husband for two years. The corpse is only the shell of the man she fell in love with and married, but the appearance is like someone tore part of him away, and not that long ago. A gaping wound on his side causes a slumped-over gait while part of the face is hanging by a small piece of flesh. White bone shows on his skull with matted hair. I gulp back rising bile imagining what made him the way he is now.

We follow the movement of the corpses for a moment and see they've breached the island wall with bodies. Nothing kept them away from the people they were meant to secure. Maybe the ramp wasn't steep enough, or maybe the piling up of bodies helped, there's no way of telling what did it, just that they made it to the living and devoured them.

It's time to go, this rescue is done. No survivors.

"Stop," Colette says, her voice only just audible over the sound of the engine. "I can't leave him like this."

"There's nothing you can do," Charlie says.

"I can give him peace." Colette reaches into the back seat of the truck with a shaking hand and pulls out my rifle. A tear crawls down her face.

I touch her arm. "Colette, you don't need to do this."

She shrugs away from me. "Yes, I do."

I pull the truck a little closer to the edge of the pit and stop, driver's side facing the mass of corpses. It's hard to make sure, but I try to keep Peter in sight. As the truck stops, Colette stares out the windshield. She's hard to read now, face placid, mouth slightly open as she breathes, waiting for her mind to make a decision on what to do. I've seen this in other raids. Hunters do it all the time. They try to dehumanize the act of killing. But these are corpses, not the living. Still, to end the existence of someone you know, even if they're not who they were before, has a toll on you. A finality to life. While Peter's body is still animated, she can torture herself with the thought he's still somehow alive. Some part of him exists and could come back to her. But it's not true. No matter what people think, the person is no more. Hell has moved in.

We wait. There is no need to rush the situation. The people are dead and there's no other leads on other survivors from the community I helped build last year. With only a few of us left, we can still go on. Survive. But to what end? I see Colette and she's about to end the final existence of the man she loved, and it reminds me we'll all end up this way. Corpses walking the Earth searching for something to eat. To devour. Searching for a pound of flesh. Something to get us through an existence without end.

And would there be anything left of me? What part of my former life would survive? Nothing, is all I can come up with. There's nothing after we're corpses. I've seen what happens to a person once they change. My friend didn't recognize me. He just saw me as meat. Nothing registered in the eyes but desire and want to feed. I can only hope someone is strong enough to do to me what Colette is about to do for her husband.

Colette still has not fired. "You okay with this?" I ask.

She snaps out of her melancholy. Sympathetic eyes turn toward me and she nods. "I'll be okay." Her voice is soft, firm, steady, resolute. She hits the window button and it slides down.

I thought she'd have gotten out and gone down to the pit. Maybe use the back of the truck bed or something. What she does is climb half way out the of the truck, and sits on the door's window frame. The thud of the bi-pod on the roof reverberates through me. Seconds pass. A minute. Two. Her right foot shakes. She's lost the nerve. This is not happening. I need to help her.

The shot splits the air – a resounding thunder clap. I look to the pit and Peter is still standing, the right side of his head missing now. The corpse staggers for a second, as if not wanting to give up even this awful existence. Then, a final lumbering step fails. It folds forward, head crashing into the ground as the remainder of his brain splatters.

The drive back took less time than getting there, but it had a silence to it that none of us wanted to break. Even though I usually like to have something playing, this time it seems inappropriate. Colette doesn't move from her seat, not even to adjust or get comfortable. She stares out the window not even pointing out vehicles or corpses. I don't blame her. No one should have to do what she did. But in our new world I doubt this was the first time such a thing happened.

Camp is still the same, the people are walking about and doing what's needed to survive. Mindy, Mom, Zoey, and I settle down for a nice meal. Mom bagged a wild turkey while we were out. Samantha eats the giblets with enthusiasm. Life appears to be good, but the meal doesn't taste the way it should. Bland in a way, but at least there's a normality to everything right now, and I bask in it, trying to divorce myself from the image of Peter. Maybe the future is not so grim as it once seemed to be. We can live, maybe even thrive. The world may have needed this reboot to put us on the right track.

I take the bowl of turnip and scoop out a good serving. Mom smiles. The evening gives a facade of perfection.

A shot echoes through our meal like a town crier through the streets. I'm up and running for the door, hand grabbing my Glock on the small table there. Mom and Mindy follow, though Mindy is more trying to run but only getting a quick walk out of it.

We're not the only ones attracted to the sound. Carl and Jill run toward the boat shed along with a few others. The newly freed women are nowhere in sight. Probably hanging low in the house we put them in. Who could blame them for not wanting to get involved with our problems. Maybe in the near future we can make them feel like part of the family but until then, we're giving them a lot of time to integrate.

Carl and Jill make it to the shed first and disappear inside it. Doc runs from his home. His oversized frame attempts to keep his belly from bouncing as he pumps his arms, slows, bends over, and wheezes out air from lungs too old for such exercise. I try to direct Mindy to him but she's not seeing it, or she's ignoring me. One of the two.

The shed is lit from a small lantern hanging from the ceiling. The kerosene antique gives off a bright light. It is a welcoming sight from the twilight of the evening. Colette is to one side of the room while Carl and Jill kneel on the ground. A body is sprawled out, not moving. It takes a second before I recognize Gretchen. There's not much left of her face, even after recovering from the torture Mom put her through. Carl is covering up the face with a rag while Jill shakes her head. There seems to be a theme happening in our lives of someone making a turn and following a path they shouldn't have to.

Mom reaches the body while Mindy puts both hands to her mouth. She didn't know the woman, none of us did. Still, the blood splatter mixed with bone and brain catches us all.

Colette is the one who grabs my attention. Inside the room she's calm and collected. Even has a small smile on her face. Wide eyes stare at the scene before her. In her right hand is a revolver, a really big one. I go to her and reach out. She doesn't stop me, only keeps the smile on her face. I take the .44 Magnum from her. Don't know where she got it from, but I piece the scene together, the why of it all crashes into my mind.

There's a smell about the muzzle of the gun and one spent round in the cylinder. She shot the woman. It seems like she did it at point blank range. Why did Gretchen not do anything like move out of the way or fight? It's execution style. A bullet to the back of the head. It comes out of the front and destroys the face if angled correctly. And it seems Colette angled it right. The blood spatter on the wall tells a tale of a sitting woman, a kneeling woman, and the shot. Hell, there's even a splintering of wood where the round hit the wall after exiting the face.

"He can rest now," Colette whispers.

I whip my head around. "What?"

"He can rest now. The bad woman is dead." She turns to me, hand coming up and touching the side of my face. Fingers stroke my cheek. "I've made it right. If they didn't attack us, Peter would be alive. A life for a life. They took him from me, I took her from them."

"You wanted revenge?" I ask.

"No, silly. I wanted peace. I wanted justice." Her voice is soft and gentle. There's a disturbing quality about it, like a child's voice after unwittingly torturing a small animal without knowing what it means. "Like the Bible says, and eye for an eye. Hammurabi's code. We live in times when we must enact our own justice using such."

I don't know the reference but the eye for an eye strikes me. "I don't want to believe in revenge."

"Not revenge, repayment of a debt. She made sure we lost people. They paid with their lives. I now take hers as payment toward her salvation." Colette hugs me. "Don't be sad, she's in a better place now."

Mom pulls Colette away from me. "We could have gotten more information from her. Put an end to all the killing. Why?"

"Eye for an eye." Colette lets out a forced laugh, her smile twitching at one corner.

Mom shakes her head. "Steve, lock her in her house and come back here. Make sure she doesn't have anything to cause any more problems." She glances at the gun in my hand. "That what she used?"

"Yes," I say. "One round spent, smells like it was just fired." I hand it over to her.

"Good, we'll need to talk to the others about what this means, but until then, just get her out of here."

I take Colette by the arm and walk her out of the shed.

She doesn't struggle, just follows, eyes not focusing on anything. This is more like the woman I met that night at Cindy's than the strong woman who grew up over the last couple of weeks. What caused her to carry out what she saw as justice? I don't know, but we need to find out if this is because of what she went through or something that will happen to all of us.

Doc gasps for air just outside the shed. He's not used to running. There's a quick glance at Colette and back to me, eyes question what's happening.

"Colette shot Gretchen," I say.

"I better get in there–"

"There's nothing you can do for her." I look at the ground. "She executed her."

Doc's eyes go wide. "No."

"Yes, one shot in the back of the head." I turn to leave, then stop, looking back at Doc. "I'm taking her back to her cabin, can you join me? I've got a lot of questions and could use your help."

"I should look in on the body."

"Nothing you can do, Doc. Her head exploded out of her face. She's dead, unless you can piece the brains together and get her going again. Besides, looks like you need to walk it off."

He flushes, then gets his breath back under control. "I'll come with you."

"Good, don't want to be the only one checking out the cabin."

We walk over to the house, or better to say cabin, that Colette has. There's a line of them, once used for staff and rented to families wanting to get away from Toronto. One big bunkhouse sits across from it. The cabin's not much, just a living room, bedroom, bathroom, and open kitchen area but it's homey. People pay a lot of money to get the feeling of being away from it all. Didn't understand why people who love nature so much wouldn't live in the country instead of in the city. We're not that far away from Toronto and the price of living there really sucked compared to out here. Air's better as well.

The cabin is clean. Too clean. A picture of Colette and Peter standing by the home they lived in and a big moving van in the background being emptied rests on a coffee table. Not sure where she got it from, but there it is. An old decorative musket hangs over the fireplace. It seems Colette finished dinner, cleaned up, and went out to shoot Gretchen. Fully premeditated. Nothing to argue about that.

There's nothing in the living room or kitchen to really cause issues.

A quick glance in the bathroom and the same thing. The bedroom appears as if she didn't sleep on the bed, but other than that, nothing is out of place. Doc sits on the small couch with Colette, talking with her about the day's events and she just smiles and lets him know what happened. After a few minutes, he pats her hand and stands, motioning me outside with a nod.

We walk out to the road and he runs a hand through thinning hair. "She's what I would call crazy."

I do a double take at him. "I thought people in your profession didn't like that word?"

"What, vets?" He laughs. "You know that's what I am, right? Oh, I can take care of people all the same, we're just animals anyway. No, she's got something wrong with her and it's a little bit out of my league to fix. Hell, I don't know if you can fix what's wrong with her."

"What should we do?"

"Nothing, she'll snap out of this or she won't. I can tell you, if she keeps falling there's–"

A bang comes from the cabin and I sprint inside. Doc follows as best he can but I'm through the door facing one of the worse things a person can ever see.

17

WILD FIRE

Colette is on the couch. A picture of her and Peter lays on her lap, blood spattered on it as a testament of their love. Her head lolls to the side and forward, blood running from an open mouth. Her right hand still grasps the musket. Smoke rolls from the warm muzzle. A crimson stain runs across the wall behind her, small bits of bone and brain dotting it with diffuse colour. A reminder of the ever presence of death in today's world. Colette is gone like so many others. But there's nothing I can do about what happened. A finality of this is beyond my understanding. She took her own life. I did see the signs of it, but ignored them believing she would not have a way of acting on them. Now she's at peace.

The muskets are show pieces Mom put in every cabin. It seems Colette knew more about firearms than she let on about. Or at least about the old flint lock ones. But there's not that much to know about them besides how to pull a trigger or load them.

Doc walks over to the body and checks for a pulse. I really don't understand why. It's obvious to me she's dead. The bullet went in her mouth and out the top of her head. Clean. No coming back from this one, not even as a corpse. I guess that's what she had in mind. We'll never know.

A flicker in the bedroom is what I'm concerned with. I walk over to the room and push open the door. Flames dance on the bed. Smoke billows into the living from the room. Crap, guess she wanted to make sure. We can't stop this, not without a fire truck or something.

"Doc, we gotta go!"

He glances toward the bedroom and stands up. "Help me get her out."

"No time," I say, grabbing his arm, head spinning. I have a family that needs to be moved to safety. Hell, everyone needs to move to safety. "This place will go up like a tinderbox. It's all dry wood."

It doesn't seem to register to him. I pull at his arm, bringing him outside.

The fire spreads across the dry wood. There's no time to waste just standing around watching it. I go to the cabin beside Colette's and hammer on the door, then to the next one. Most of the trees in the forest are still dry from the winter, sap not yet up into the branches. We're in a situation now that none of us foresaw. We could lose the camp. In fact, we could lose the whole area around it as well. Mom said there were others in the woods with campers and such. We need to get them all out.

"Get the women," I yell at doc. "This fire may spread fast and then it'll cut us off from the road!"

Doc does his fast run-walk to the main building, the out-cabin as we call it. This is where the women we rescued were put to kept them safe. They all have their own rooms and keys to each one, giving them a measure of security. We thought it would help them feel safe to have control over their lives. Hope we weren't wrong. But this will put them on high alert. At least it's Doc and not me rushing into their sanctuary.

I hammer on the door of the final cabin as the last of the sun's light leaves the area. Darkness is not a good time to do this but we have no choice. A shadow effect shows against the door and I look over to see the fire spread to the outside of the cabin and a few trees now sporting dancing flames.

The door opens with Charlie standing there, a woman in a bathrobe behind him.

"What the fuck!" He stares past me at the building wildfire. Flames are now reaching up to the sky on some of the trees.

"We need to get out of here. Grab what you can and meet me at the trucks," I say, and run off to follow Doc.

The door to the main cabin is open and I run into it. The reception area of the camp is large, and with that a dining area to the right. Doc has the women all standing about waiting. My rush in causes them to flinch a little but there's no time for niceties.

"There's a fire. We need to go." I rush past them and to the front door. Some of the people are coming through the woods near Mom's house and pointing at the cabin behind us. Zoey is running out, carrying a screaming Samantha in her arms.

"Get to the truck!" I yell at Zoey.

She takes the hint. When I'm this excited she knows to just do what I say. She heads to the first truck she sees, gets in, and closes the door. Samantha jumps from her arms. My cat stares at the fire in the distance through the rear window.

I run toward the shed, telling people to get their stuff and meet us at the trucks. Most listen, some want to ask questions but I just keep running toward the shed.

Mom is rushing toward the parking area as our home goes up in flames around us. The fire behind the cabin spreads quickly. Black smoke from the pine needles drifts into the sky. It's like a beacon to the world – we're here.

I reach Mom and she grasps my arms. "What happened?"

"Colette," I gasp out. "She killed herself and lit the cabin on fire. Now the forest is lighting up from all the pine needles."

"We need to get people out of here." She lets go of my arms. "We don't have time to waste with anyone." She stops and turns. "Where's Zoey?"

"In one of the trucks with Samantha." I run to the shed, yelling out behind me, "I'll get Mindy."

Everyone who was in the shed now stands outside watching the growing light in the west. The blaze picks up; we need to get out of the area. I see Mindy, she's my first concern. Then I catch Carl and Jill. Good, they will know what to do. It only takes a second to explain what happened and they organize the other's to hit the back woods were the campers are. They need to hit the road through their emergency exit and meet us at the Community Centre. We set that as the first rendezvous.

I put Mindy in the truck with Zoey and head to where I last saw Mom. She's there, but ducking into the main cabin for some reason. The fire grows closer like a beast reaching out to us and I worry about how much time we really have. The pine needles are working as an accelerant, spreading the fire faster than I can imagine.

"Stay here," I say to Mindy and Zoey as I jump out of the truck. A quick sprint takes me to the front entrance of the main cabin and there is Mom with Doc and the women. "I said to get them out!"

"Steve, settle down. We have time," Mom says. "We need to organize this better."

"The hell with that," I say. "We need to leave, now."

Mom turns to Doc. "Well?"

"Yes, we do have to leave." Doc glances at me. "Steve, you take some of the women and I'll get the rest. We need to keep our group together. Your mom is coming with me."

I can't believe what he's saying. "Mom, come with me right now so we can get you out of here."

"I'm going with Tom." She steps toward the women. "You three there, go with Steve. You other two, go with him as well. Just get into the flat bed and stay low."

"Mom!"

"You heard me. Take those girls and get them to safety." She turns to Doc. "Tom and I will meet you at the Community Centre."

"Fuck," I mutter. "Come on!" I say to the women.

We exit the cabin and help the women into the back of the truck. I climb in and one of the girls, an older one of about twenty-five, climbs into the back with Zoey.

Mindy glances about the faces. "Where's your Mom?"

"She's getting a ride with Doc," I say, and start the truck. "Don't ask. I don't know a damn thing."

I slam the vehicle into reverse and turn around. The main road into the camp runs next to trees already on fire. There's a better choice than braving the fire and possibly killing the women in the back. I turn us around and head out the back way behind Mom's house.

We wait in the parking lot of the Community Centre north of the camp. My hope is the road will work as a fire stop. Only a few corpses litter the area, not hard to take out. Maybe the horde gathered up the ones in the area and only stragglers stayed. Anyway, people take an easy breath as they pass by me and the rifle. I figure we could stay here until everyone is safe and sound.

Carl and Jill pull up right behind us, the rest of the women in the back of their truck. Some stragglers come in after them in large mobile homes and converted trucks. Most run well but the odd one has problems. Two have flat tires and Carl does his best to help out.

Charlie pulls up in the last truck with a few people in the back. He glances about, as if searching for someone. The lift in his step is not the same as it was before, but at least it seems he has a girlfriend. I take a closer look. It's Cindy. Crap, I would never have taken him for someone who liked older women, just too active a person. But here he is with someone well into their sixties if not older.

I count the vehicles: the three trucks, four big campers, and five converted trucks. We could put a couple of the girls in each of the campers and spread out the load. It'd be better than them holding up in the back of the trucks.

The Community Centre is never locked. I get someone with a flashlight to follow me in and we make sure it's clear of corpses. Cots decorate the floor. advanced planning from a week ago. Good thing we did, they're needed now. Most will sleep in their campers or trailers, but the rest of us need a place to hunker down for the night.

A lot of questions are asked, but I just tell them to hold on. We can figure out what needs to happen in the morning. I need sleep, and this day's been a long one. There are no answers right now, and I couldn't figure one out if it slapped me in the face. One night's sleep will help me decide what to do. It will also give Mom and Doc time to reach us.

I set up cots for Mindy, Zoey, and myself in the foyer. Samantha bugs to be let out but I decide its best to keep her in with us. I don't want to have to run around chasing a cat with all the shit that's happened in our world. My head hits the pillow and I stare at the ceiling. Mindy lies in the cot beside me.

"It's been a while since we haven't slept together," she says.

"Not if you don't count the times either of us was abducted."

She laughs. "What do you think?"

"About what?"

"Where we're going?"

Shit, not her as well. "I haven't given it much thought." I roll over to look in her direction. "We could try and make for high ground but that gives us a problem with the people in campers. Most of them won't make it up that steep a hill. Then, we have all the people we need to find places for. The women in the mobiles may get the wrong idea and think they're back with the biker's way of life. I don't want that to happen. We have few choices."

"Do you think Doc and Mom will come?"

"I don't know. It's too much to wonder about tonight. I need to sleep."

"Okay, but figure something out. The group is looking to you for answers and a lot of them are scared."

Great, answers. Everyone wants answers to questions and I have no idea what to tell them. We tried living in our own homes and look what that got us. I tried to get everyone together at my mom's camp and that just blew up in our faces. We need an answer for this problem and I'm just a system administrator in a world with no computers trying to make his way through life. What more could people ask of me? Why the hell am I still alive when people far more knowledgeable than me are dead? How did this all happen in the first place?

I don't think the answer will come to me tonight, but I sure as hell need to figure some of them out.

I toss and turn. Try to get some sleep but the thought of having to find a place for all of us keeps screaming in my head. We need a place to stay that is safe. Check, I figured that one out this morning, the only problem is getting there. We also need to make sure we have food to eat. Figured that one out as well. Lots of food where I think we should go. It'll be hard at first, but I'm sure we'll be able to live a good long life full of fun and enjoyment. I'll have to run this past all the others and see what they think.

We should be safe in the new location but that's something we'll need to figure out.

The morning takes forever to come as I stare at the ceiling with sleeping people around me. Mindy snores lightly beside me and Zoey tosses and turns on the other side. Samantha jumps on me when the light leaks into the foyer. She lands on my full bladder and I struggle to stay down. Her heavy paws walk up and she settles down on my chest, nose sniffing at my chin. Her bristled tongue slides against my morning scruff.

I put my arms around her and sit up, swinging my feet over the side of the cot. It must be around five, maybe a little earlier. The light from outside is diffused and gives little help to find my way around the area. Samantha rests on my shoulder, letting me pet her. The rumbling from her is soothing. The hall has a bathroom to the side but on opening it, there's no light. Probably no water pressure either. Some of the people brought flashlights, while other's had matches. A stench lingers in the air and I close the door hoping people are not using the place for it's intended purpose.

Outside is probably the best place to relieve myself. I put Samantha down and exit the building, making my way to the north side of the centre.

The overcast sky threatens to release rain on us, otherwise it's a pleasant enough spring morning. Probably late May, but I've lost track of the days since the world went to hell. I keep trying to make sense of what happened but it's not coming together as I hoped.

Now, out of the way and out of sight of anyone, I unzip relieve myself. I don't remember drinking so much water but I did. The world is a strange place; we wake up, go to the bathroom, eat, love, and do it all over again the next day. We will be that way again soon. As soon as we are safe again.

A hand rests on my shoulder, fingers grip, and weight leans on me. People do strange things when they see others doing something different.

"No light inside. Just give me a second."

The smell of rotting flesh drifts. Another hand drops onto my shoulder just as the last of the urine leaves my body. I look down to see a half rotted hand resting there. Urine almost starts to flow again. My stomach tightens as I glance up and see the face coming closer. It looks different but still wanting. The top of the mouth hits my back but nothing else. I jump away. The lower jaw is missing from the face. The arm comes away from the body as I pull back further. Bile rises in my throat. The corpse topples forward, flesh all but rotted. The bony hand lets go and falls to the ground, the other arm dangles from the body on a few sinews. There are no eyes in the skull. Nothing.

I reach out and push the corpse away. Two steps back and it tumbles, falling to the ground. The head breaks away as the back slams against the pavement. It rolls forward, coming to a halt with the back facing me. All the skin is gone, left on the ground behind it.

Another corpse walks out of the treeline to the North West. McFarland Street, some of the largest homes in Ballantrae. It's strange they've been in there all this time and nothing has happened to them. The stumbling body comes forward, not in a straight line, but somewhat looping around, stopping, sniffing the air, then walking again. As it gets closer skin hanging from its body sways, entrails hang out from the stomach, swaying with each clumsy step.

A shot rings out, striking the corpse in the head. It falls to the ground.

I spin around and see Carl standing there with Jill's AR in his hands. He glares at me for a second, then lowers it, and starts to walk toward me.

"What the hell are you doing, Steve?"

"I was just taking a piss." I motion to the back of the centre. "Didn't think anyone else was going to be out here."

"Lucky I was." Carl flips the safety on. "What's the problem?"

"With what?"

He points to the corpse. "You just watched that thing come toward you. Why?"

"I wanted to get a better look at it."

"Why?"

"I'll show you."

I take him behind the centre and show him the one that tried to attack me. He takes it in, but seems to miss some of the fine points. I toe the head around and point out the missing eyes. We then walk to the other corpse.

"The eyes are missing on this one also." Carl scratches his head. "What the hell."

"The skin is falling off it as well. Maybe they're rotting a little faster than we thought they would?"

"But what does that mean?" I push the corpse, trying to turn it over a little more, but the intestines fall out and break apart. The smell hits both of us hard, making me gag.

"What the hell are you two doing?" Mindy calls out, breaking the silence.

18

LOOK WHO'S HERE

I spin around to see Mindy standing at the corner of the centre with Mom and Doc beside her. The light of the morning reflects off her mess of hair. I don't think she's ever looked so beautiful. Something about seeing her in the morning light excites me. At this time, I believe there is a God out there somewhere, and I thank him or her for allowing us to find one another.

Seeing Mom and Charlie lifts my heart. I worried about them through the night, not knowing what happened or if there was going to be another hole in my life. The flood of feelings for Mom breaks down a barrier, one I built up long ago.

"Mom," I utter.

In another unnatural show of emotion, Mom steps forward as I rush toward her. My arms encircle her small frame and she squeezes me back. "I thought…"

"Not this time," she says.

Her body stiffens a little. I let go, allowing my arms to linger on her shoulders as she blushes, looking at the people around us. Finally, I let her go, reach out, and shake Doc's hand. I don't know what's going on between them, but if he had anything to do with the reason she stayed behind all night we're going to have some words. He won't like it much, but at least he'll know where he stands as far as my mother goes.

"Good to see you again, Steve." His grip is tight, eyes still the gentle sort I'm used to seeing on him. Something tells me to be a little warier of him, but that could just be the son in me.

"Glad you didn't get yourself dead," I say, smiling at him. "We need to talk, soon."

"No, you two don't need to talk soon," both Mindy and Mom say.

I look at both of them just as Doc does. Not sure what they're thinking, but when it comes to Mom I'm going to be a little protective. I give Doc a nod and he seems to understand.

"Where have you been?"

Doc blushes more and Mom points to the parking lot. "Had to get the old girl. Wouldn't leave her back there to die in the fire."

As if to compound it, I see Mom's old Mercedes GL350, a diesel SUV. The thing still looks brand new. "Where the hell were you hiding that thing?"

"I'm surprised you didn't run into it out back of the house! It's been in a little shed out there." Mom looks away. She lifts a hand to cover her mouth, as if it will muffle her whispered words. "Behind all the other stuff and covered with a tarp."

"Crap, we could have used that weeks ago," I say.

"And have her shot up? Right. Not going to happen. I'm the only one who drives her." She holds out the keys, then snatches them away before I can snatch them. "Anyway, I grabbed what I could out of the kitchen. We have some canned food and such to feed the people. Did you remember to bring any?"

I shake my head. Mindy comes to my rescue.

"The campers have food. They'll also have ways of cooking it. Did you bring a stove?" Mindy folds her arms.

"I'm that child's grandmother, and don't you forget it," Mom says and walks to the SUV.

Doc shakes his head and follows her. I put my arm around Mindy's shoulders and pull her tight. "I know there's a reason I love you."

"Besides the great sex?" she asks.

"That's what I was talking about."

People start waking up about an hour after Mom arrives. Most heard the shot but since there was no follow up, I guess they surmised it was nothing to worry about. We move chairs and tables out of the Community Centre and start making breakfast until the sky decides we need a shower. Rain comes down on us and we move back inside. Campers park on the grass near the entrance to gain easier access to the building, and all the cots are moved aside to make several large community tables.

Mindy sits opposite me, and Zoey is to my left. Carl and Jill sit to my right. Doc sits between Mom and Mindy. We eat in quiet contemplation of what happened yesterday. The fire and Colette are at the front of my thoughts. The basic understanding of what she did and why keeps coming up, but understanding it does not.

"I don't know what went through her mind," Doc says as he pushes some of the re-hydrated egg around his plate.

"We'll never know," Jill says. "People just crack. I know I would have if Steve hadn't found me."

Mindy looks at me. "I think most people feel you've helped them."

My cheeks heat up. "Just doing what's right." At least I hope I am.

Mom pushes her plate away. "Most people don't do things like that, what's right I mean. Take a look at the bikers. They could've been really good for people. Heck, they were organized and able to do what was needed. Now, they're a mess with Pa dead. I'll be surprised they can keep going after being kicked in the ass by us."

Zoey pushes beans around on her plate. She's bored, and only three other kids are here, all of them in campers. I put my hand on her head. "You can go play if you want to."

She hugs me and runs from the table. To be a child again, that would be a treasure. Not having to worry about what all us adults worry about and still have time to play.

"Where are we going?" The question from Mom hits everyone, and it needs an answer.

"I was thinking Simcoe. If we can find a way to Snake Island, maybe we'll be okay there."

"Thorah Island would be better," Mom says. "Less population and not owned by the Chippewas. We may be able to find something to take us across in Beaverton."

"I'd rather not spend that much time on the road." I push my plate away.

"If the Band survived, you'll have a fight on your hands with Snake Island. They never relinquished it." Mom scoops the last of her eggs into her mouth.

"Beaverton is a long way away. Maybe we should put it to a vote." I push away from the table and stand. All the adults in our group are here. I realize some people didn't follow us from the camp, wanting to take their own chances at survival. "Can I have everyone's attention for a second."

The room quiets down and all eyes focus on me. I hate being the centre of attention in a large group, but this is a necessary evil if we're going to survive. "The fire knocked out a lot of the cabins. With those shelters destroyed, we need to find another place to live. I know some of yo–"

"Maybe the camp's not destroyed," someone yells out. I look around and spot the man. Overweight, flesh filled out on his round face. Probably in his early thirties.

"It's gone," Mom says, her voice causing a ripple effect with the crowd.

"We could still park on the south end of the property." A woman's voice this time.

"Go ahead," Mom says. "The fire took out most of the trees. I'm sure the corpses won't mind if you're easy to spot."

"Look, people, we need to figure out what we're going to do to survive." I turn to Mom and give her a pleading look.

I glance about the room and fifty odd pairs of eyes stare back at me. "The good thing is our small group is easy to take care of. That's also bad because we now have to all step up and watch everywhere in order to be safe. I'm thinking we should make our way to one of the islands in Simcoe." People look at each other. "If we go to one of the islands, there'll be no reason to worry about the corpses coming at us, and anyone else will need to figure out how to cross over to get what we have."

The talking picks up. People have questions, but I have no answers. They all speak at once, shouting out what they want to know in order to be heard. It doesn't help, and I can't tell who is asking what.

"Hold on everyone!" I hold up my arms. "You all have questions. I may not be able to answer them. Help me out here, one at a time, please."

They do so, firing questions up at me and I try to answer them as best as possible. It comes across as a good sharing session of my ideas and what they can think of. When it all settles, we have a consensus of what we're doing, though I'm not happy with some of it. I first thought Snake Island would be the best goal, but someone fished on Simcoe and there's a large native presence on it, along with Fox Island. Thorah is the one the group likes. No natives to worry about and we only have to concern ourselves with getting there from Beaverton. In the winter, a natural ice bridge is formed on the water and we'd have easy access to the town without much worry about corpses due to the winter freeze. There's also a harbour which could house a barge. It would make life easier if we had access to that as well.

Mitch, one of the fishermen, mentioned the barge should be diesel, depending on how old the thing is. It's his belief the age of the vessel is greater than I would have thought. It left us with only one last thing to talk about, how to get into the town safely. Knowing that using a lot of guns would attract more corpses than we may have the ability to handle, we decided to go in with bows. There's only a few of us handy with them, and that includes Mindy. I argued against it, but she insisted, citing exactly what was mentioned before, we're short people who can use them. I'm not happy with that, but there's nothing I can do to stop her. Mindy has a mind of her own.

Mom knows the area the best, so I use her knowledge to help us out.

"The Bowmen club is on McCowan north of here," she says. "You can raid the club and get bows and arrows for everyone. For better than regular bows, you'll need to find someplace else, like one of the club member's places. They'll have records there."

"You could help us find the records. I'm sure some of them will be in an office or something."

She glances at Doc but he looks away. There's something she's not telling us and I want to know what it is. "We're not going."

"What'd you mean, you're not going?"

She stands, takes my hand. "We're not going. I know a few places to find out some information. Places from when I was in CSIS that need to be checked." She drops my hand. "Doc and I will go to them and meet you at the island."

I understand her statement; it's the why that fails to register. "I can come with you. Carl and Jill could help out–"

"It's not that easy," Mom says. "The place we need to go to is in Toronto."

I close the door to Mom's SUV once she's inside. Doc gets into the passenger side and puts on his seat belt. I can't help but laugh a little as he keeps pulling to get it around his girth.

"I didn't do it on the drive over and the beeping drove me insane," Doc says. "Besides, we'll be doing a lot of dodging on the road into Toronto."

Mom puts her belt on as well. She doesn't start the vehicle, not yet. Her hands grip the steering wheel, knuckles turning white. Something is going on and she hasn't told me what it is. I'm concerned enough to say something, but don't know what it should be.

"I haven't been to Toronto for a long time," she finally says. "I bet it's changed."

"Don't take the highways," I say. "They're probably all choked up with cars and accidents. Try to take the side roads, stay off the mains if you can. And don't worry if you need to drive on someone's lawn to get to where you're going, I'm sure they won't mind."

She looks at me, eyebrows raised and a slight smile touches the corner of her mouth. This is the look I want to burn into my memory. The one of my mom being happy, entertained, alive. Something tells me I may not see either of them after they leave.

"I'm going to the Public Health Agency wing of the CSIC building downtown. There's no lawns, except the one in the Parliament building, and I'll be a little bit north of that." She puts the key into the ignition and turns over the engine. "Did you hear the station again?"

I shake my head. "The last time was when I came back with Colette."

"Listen to it. They changed the language they've been transmitting with. I think this time it's French."

She turns on the station, and yes, the language has changed to French.

"Think they'll use English next?" I ask.

"Maybe," she says. "If you don't listen, you'll never know."

There's nothing to do but nod at the statement.

Mindy comes up beside me and leans in, giving Mom a kiss on the cheek. "You take care of that old fart sitting beside you."

"I will. You take care of that child growing inside you."

"I will," Mindy says. "Doc, you gotta come back and deliver my baby, you hear?"

"Sure will, Mindy," he says with a smile. "Just make sure we have something to come back to."

"Remember, the archery club and then Thorah Island. We'll make our way there once we've finished with what I need to do."

I pull out my Glock and hand it to her. She stares at it for a few seconds and hands it back.

"You need something," I say.

"Already got that covered." She opens the arm rest and pulls out a MAC-10 machine pistol. "This has more rounds and fires faster than yours."

"That's cheating. Gotta give the corpses a better chance than that." I put my Glock back in the holster. "How long you think it's going to take to get what you need?"

She sighs. "A couple of days. Probably take all day to get down there and another few days to search what we need. You never know, Doc could find the cause of this curse and a cure before we return."

Doc humphs beside her.

Mom reaches over and takes his hand. "Could be worse, I could be riding with a realist."

We both laugh at that. Doc just shakes his head.

"I'd feel better if you take some more people with you." I motion to Carl and Jill. "Just say the word and I bet they'd go with you."

"No, just the two of us. That way if something goes wrong all I have to worry about is Doc here." She scratches his double chin. "Maybe I'll make him jog behind the truck for some exercise as well."

"I can get out here, you know," Doc says.

"I'm only kidding you." Mom smiles at the man.

I just shake my head. "Okay, but remember, we'll be on the island and watching the shoreline for you."

"Best to just leave a radio or something. We'll see it and call you." She takes out a small note pad and scribbles on it. "Take this and tune to that frequency on the sideband of channel nine. I'll monitor it with one of the rigs I'll pick up from the centre."

"CB radio? No one has those anymore." I glance at the paper and put it in my pocket.

"You'll be surprised. Just pick a big boat and you'll see one in it. Maybe even the barge they talked about this morning." She puts the SUV into drive. "I'll see you soon, Steven. Take care of Mindy and my grandchild while I'm gone."

I step back and she drives the truck out of the parking lot onto the road. My hand is up, waving. There's a finality to the situation. My mother is gone, again. And this time it's she who's leaving, not me. We didn't do anything wrong, she just decided now, after a whole year, to check out downtown for any clues on what is happening to our broken world.

Mindy puts her arm around me. "She'll be back. I know it."

"I won't be so sure," I say, squeezing her into me.

***

Zoey sits on her coat holding Samantha like a rag doll. I'm not sure why the cat lets her do that but it's the sweetest thing in the world to see. My cat's front paws are sticking out from her body and the soft underbelly fur is being stroked by Zoey's free hand.

As I walk up to her cot, Samantha struggles free and struts to the end of the cot to groom herself. It's been eight hours since Mom and Doc left. People are getting ready to leave and we have a small group who will take on the job of getting the bows. This time, Mindy and I are going to travel with the group and stay out of the way. It's only a little ways away, but there's no reason for everyone to go with Carl and Jill. We'll just wait out on the road for them to finish what's needed and come back.

"I want a cat, too," Zoey says.

"Sorry?" It's all I can think of saying.

"I want a cat, too," Zoey repeats. "Samantha's your cat, and I want one just like her."

I glance at Samantha as she licks her stomach. "She's not really my cat, just a companion. And it seems she likes being around you, as well."

Zoey grins. "Then she's my cat, too?"

I grin. "No, more like we are her guardians."

"Gadines? What's that?"

I keep forgetting how young Zoey is. She must not have finished much school, maybe kindergarten or something like that. "That's when someone looks out for another. Like Mindy and I do with you."

Zoey seems to accept that with a nod. "I'm Samantha's gadine."

This little girl makes me laugh, but there's more to life than playing and eating. We'll have to start teaching her things like reading and math. Can't let the world die out of spite.

"How'd you like to learn stuff, starting tomorrow?" I say, picking her up in a hug. "We can teach you how to do math and read and write."

"Okay," she says, her small arms going around my neck in a hug. "Can Bobby join us?"

"Sure, Bobby can join us, but not for tomorrow, he's a little older than you and we'll need to get you up to his level." I put her on the bed and pull up the sheets. "It's time for you to go to sleep now."

Zoey yawns. "But I don't want to go to sleep."

"I know, baby, but tomorrow will come sooner than you think."

19

THE POINTY END

I'm a little nervous. People are packing up and not thinking of the how difficult it's going to be getting to the island. Maybe they're optimistic with the plan. I don't know. We need to get the bows and move out fast. The problem is the logistics of keeping fifteen-odd vehicles together with all the crap on the road. What one truck has no problem manoeuvring around another will need to find an alternate route for. Especially these large campers some of them have. Hopefully they all have enough fuel to not worry about the trip, those campers get horrible gas mileage.

Mindy comes up beside me, snuggles into my body, and leans her head on my chest. I put an arm around her, squeeze her small shoulders.

She lifts her head to look at me. "We'll be okay, right?"

"Should be." My voice is steady, not like my insides. Too much has happened for me to not worry about everyone and us. "Is Zoey ready?"

"She's already in the truck with Samantha. She really loves that ball of fur."

I kiss the top of Mindy's head. "It's good to know."

"Steve, is this place going to be the right place for us? I mean, will we be safe?"

What can I say to that? No, the place is going to be hell on Earth just like all the places around us. The truth sucks, but how would I know that for sure? An island. Almost two kilometres away from the main land. We *should* be safe. If not, then where would we find shelter?

"We'll be safe." I squeeze and let go.

Too many people to worry about. And with Mom leaving, the proverbial torch of leadership lands in my hands with everyone looking to me for guidance.

I walk over to Carl and Jill's truck. They've got all their gear stowed away. Only two rifles are in the vehicle and four Glocks sit on the dash. I want to warn them not to be greedy when hitting the archery club, to be safe, and get out if there's any sign of trouble. But then, I'm only being a mother hen. It was only a short time ago I thought I'd lost both of them along with Mindy. Now they hustle like no other. It's like Carl has a mental checklist he's sharing with Jill in order to get ready. Neither of them seems to say much.

"Well?" I ask.

Jill looks up from tying something down in the back. "Just about. A couple more things to go and we'll head out."

"I'm concerned." I lean against the truck. "I don't think you two should go alone."

"We talked about this last night," Carl says. "We're running in and back out. Grab bows and arrows. Nothing too fancy."

"I know. It's just that"–I kick at a stone–"every time we plan something and it seems too easy there's problems. This time I want to be sure. I want two more people to go in with you. And I'm coming as well."

Carl stops what he's doing. "There's no reason for it."

"There's every reason. First, with more hands we can get more bows, more arrows. Second, you'll have someone watching your back if there does happen to be a problem. Third, if a door's locked, that gives another hand finding a way in. They have a kitchen in there and God only knows what we could use from their stores."

"Your mom had chickens at the camp. Why not capture some chickens?" Jill says. "We could farm on the island for all we know."

It's part of my plan, but until we have the island, there's nothing to survive on until plants start to grow under our guidance. "I'm not arguing with you. We're coming whether you like it or not."

Carl returns to his mental checklist. "Can't change your mind?"

"No."

"Then you better be ready. We're leaving now."

Charlie and I follow Carl and Jill across Aurora Road, turn right on McCowan, and head north. Abandoned vehicles cause us to swerve and corpses walk aimlessly, like they've lost their way from the horde. We almost miss the club. Metal gates bar the entrance next to a sun bleached sign. There's seven cars parked in the lot and maybe a dozen corpses wandering around the property. One big club house stands out.

We park, grab our bows, and try to kill the corpses around us. They all fall after some time, even the one poorly dressed as Friar Tuck. A few of them have bows, but the things are so weathered we decide not to bother collecting them.

I try the door to the clubhouse. It's unlocked, and the other at the back of the building is closed. I pull it open and Carl dashes through, scanning from left to right as he enters. He lets an arrow loose. "Clear."

Jill and Charlie follow and I bring up the rear. The clubhouse is spacious, with couches and one corpse sporting an arrow through the eye. Carl's getting better with that thing. Couches and tables litter the place with cups and glasses on them, most turned over. One wall has a sign near the door – Indoor Range. That's where we want to go.

Charlie snaps his fingers. He's pointing to the sign as well.

"I don't think you have to worry about someone being around here, Charlie," I say in a hushed voice. "Just keep it down and we'll be okay."

"Sorry Steve, first real raid."

We step to the range door. A small corridor with a cloak room to the left. The smell in the place reeks of mould and mildew. A hand reaches out of the room to grasp at Jill. Three arrows fly, two hit their mark.

"Christ, Charlie. I thought you practised this." I step to the body and pull out two arrows. "We have to get everyone good with these things or we'll need to make plenty of runs into a sporting goods store, if we can find one."

Charlie blushes and walks into the room to locate his arrow. I hand the other one I picked up over to Carl. Jill seems to have two guardian angels with her today.

"Thanks," she says. Her eyes fall past me and go wide.

A scream chills me. I spin. Carl lets another arrow fly. Charlie slumps down on the floor, blood gushing out of his neck. On top of him is a corpse with one arm. The other is in Charlie's hands. It must have been behind the coats or something. An arrow finds its mark in the corpse's head and it slumps. I run over the Charlie.

With a hand trying to stop the blood flow, Charlie sits up. "Shit! Mother fucker!"

There's hardly any red between his fingers so at least it's not an arterial bleed. Still, any bite is bad. Everyone who's been bitten has turned in a day if not sooner. Another person injured on my watch. Helplessness floods through me.

"Let me see," I say to Charlie.

"No need, it got me." He lifts his hand to show the bite. Must sting like a bitch.

"We can get you back to camp," Carl suggests.

"No, we don't have the time, really."

He's being stronger than I would at what happened. I help Charlie stand. He's weak, but able to balance once on his feet. Whatever it is that turns people must already be working in his blood. "We can patch you up for now. Get finished here, then clean out the wound."

"No, too late for that." He cringes. "I can feel it in me, whatever it is. Trying to get me to slow down."

Jill puts her hand on his arm. "What do you need us to do?"

She's always the sensible one. Carl and I would spend hours trying to get Charlie to relax while we try to find something to help him out. Jill knows it's too late for that, just like Carl and I know. Charlie is dead; it's just his body that doesn't realize it. Puss forms in the wound, faster than I've seen it happen in the past.

"Let me catch my breath for a second and I'll go outside."

"No, you can't do that!" The words are out of my mouth before I can stop them.

"Steve, I'm dead already. The bite is deep enough and no one gets to live after something like this. We both know it." He takes a deep breathe, hands shaking. "I'll go outside and travel east for a bit, making enough noise to draw whatever's in area away from here for you. It'll buy you guys some time to collect all the bows you can." He smiles. "That way you can tell Cindy I died bravely."

No one dies bravely. They either fight to live or give up. Charlie is sacrificing what little life he has left. Essentially giving up. He's admitted there's nothing we can do to save him, so an air of bravado is to make us feel better. For some reason I don't call him on it, just smile, and hope my eyes don't betray the way I feel.

"I'll let her know you thought of her in the end." He wavers and I reach out to steady him.

"Give them hell, Charlie," Carl says.

A tear tugs at the corner of Jill's eye. "We'll miss you."

He nods, gives a small smile, and walks toward the door, gun in hand. Just as he grasps the knob, he turns his head to look over one shoulder. A slight smile crosses his lips.

"Today is a good day to die," he says in a good Klingon accent.

I turn away as he goes outside. The door closes with finality. We're all silent, staring at the ground.

Carl clears his throat. "We need to do this."

We all turn to face the exit. Through the glass we don't see much. A line of windows at the end of the range allow enough light in to say we can go, but after what happened with Charlie, we're all gun shy. Carl breaks the silence first. His hand drops down on the latch and he pushes open the door. Not much is different in here than the club room. Jill shoots a corpse as we enter. I didn't even see it. A bank of bows lines the right side with quivers already packed beside them. Nice, not much thinking to do now. We grab the gear. The simple wood ones are good enough. No need to get fancy for the group. These will easily stop anything short of a vehicle.

I sling five and pull eight quivers. Now I'm loaded. Carl grabs one more bow but one less quiver. Jill slings her third bow but stops as gunshots sound in the distance. The eerie silence of the day amplifies everything. Charlie is drawing the corpses away.

"We got enough, let's go." I spin and head for the door, my two friends following.

Outside, a corpse lumbers into the forest. Either it's all dressed up or the thing was once the biggest man I'd ever seen. A shot fires again and its shoulder barely moves. Must be Charlie doing that.

I don't want to interrupt, but I also want to give Charlie a chance to get some distance into the woods. With one arrow nocked, I aim and let fly. It travels true, and strikes the back of the corpses head. The arrow bounces off, leaving a mar on the skull behind it. Something's wrong here. I nock another one and pull back as far as I can. This will be over thirty kilos of pull weight. I let loose the arrow. It strikes a little lower and penetrates.

The lumbering beast turns. It's wearing a football jersey and helmet, all covered in mud. No wonder the arrow didn't penetrate the skull. It teeters a little, the arrow having driven right through the base of the neck. Charlie now has time to get away, even though we're now the target for the football corpse.

Carl shakes his head while Jill just stares at the absurdity of it all. We've never seen anything like this and I hope we never will again, but it comes toward us. I'm reminded of the old Frankenstein movie with Boris Karloff and the lumbering movements he did to bring the creature to life. This bears a resemblance to it. I nock another arrow.

With the corpse walking toward me, the head is no longer protected by the helmet. I let loose the arrow and hit the thing in the brow just above its left eye. The body slumps. It hits the ground hard. Dark liquid seeps from under the helmet and the smell of rotten meat and cooked feces is so strong I gag.

"Oh God!" Jill cries out, eyes watering.

"Fuck, that one reeks!" Carl slaps a hand over his mouth. "Let's get out of here before I start to taste it."

We jump into our trucks and drive back to the Community Centre one man short.

We've all came to expect it. The loss of someone we know hits everyone in camp. Cindy stares at me blankly, seeing nothing, not even the blood on my hands and shirt from trying to help Charlie. After a few seconds she walks away, leaving me wondering if she's going to be okay or not. I ask Mindy to take care of her before we leave, make sure she eats and is ready to go when we pack up.

Zoey sits in the truck. Samantha followed her inside and seems to be tolerating the attention from the kid. Who would have thought my loner cat likes children?

We've handed out all the bows and given a quiver to everyone. Not sure if all of them can shoot, but at least they'll not feel left out. We'll handle the basics of bowman ship on the island when we have more time. With everyone together and no worry about corpses, it'll mean more people will be able to hunt. Ducks should be coming in soon, and that means water fowl for dinner. I never get tired of eating duck.

We need to keep the people together. This is the only way we have a chance to survive. I've kept myself in the shadows for years, and now everyone looks to me for direction. When will it ever end? I'm not a leader, nowhere close as far as I'm concerned.

The Community Centre is almost cleaned out. We've taken a number of the cots and tables; you never know when you'll need them. Mindy tells me Cindy is in Carl and Jill's truck. We're ready to leave. That's when I realize how much time has passed with me staring at Samantha and Zoey in the truck.

Mindy turns to me. "Is anything wrong?"

"No, nothing." I pull out the keys. "You want to drive? I'd like to rest for a little bit."

"Sure."

She takes the keys and I open the passenger door. "We don't have to go fast, just make sure there's enough space for the vehicles to get around anything."

Mindy stops and gives me a blank-faced look from the other side of the truck, her hand on the door handle.

"We also want to make sure there's enough diesel in the tank. Should be, we filled it up a couple of days ago." I glance over at her. "What you waiting for?"

"I had driving instructors who gave me less directions then you are now. You drive, I'm going to play in the back with Zoey." She tosses me the keys.

Guess I had that coming. Maybe in the next life I'll learn how to keep my big mouth shut.

I slide over the centre consul and push the key into the ignition. The truck turns over right away. Mindy gets in and immediately scratches Samantha under the chin. The purring begins.

Others have started their vehicles. I put the truck into drive. We can now begin our trip to the island. It's only fifty kilometres but who knows what we'll find.

We take forty-eight North and it curves under Simcoe. The road is clear most of the way with a few cars to either side or in the ditch. At one intersection I use the truck to push cars clear for the larger vehicles and watch corpses shuffle toward us. We get through and leave them to lumber behind us. The question is, where did all the people go? The horde that travelled north last week was the largest pack I'd ever seen. Why are there no others? Maybe the idea about the lake protecting us is correct, and we don't have to worry about it anymore. Or they are getting caught up in their migration patterns and going around the major areas with obstacles. No, there has to be a reason. Something else is driving them.

Zoey sings to Samantha in the back.

"You know what I miss the most?" Mindy asks.

The corner of my mouth lifts. "What is there to miss?"

I think about that; what is there really to miss form the old world? War? We had that. Crime? Happened as well. Government? No one misses government. But it does come to me. "Pizza."

Zoey perks up. "Pissa?"

"Oh, I could go for a garden pizza." Mindy looks out the driver's window. "Oh, I see."

Zoey stops singing. "What?"

"Pizza store over there. That's what you were thinking about."

Zoey presses her face against the window. "Can we stop?"

I look through the front of the store and see shadow's moving about. We could stop, but who'd want to eat out of the store they need to kill the occupants in order to get an order? "Don't think that's a good idea, hon."

Zoey goes back to playing with Samantha. She has a string and is dangling it for the cat to bat back and forth. At least she's not howling like when I used to take her to the vet.

Normality grabs onto our existence and takes over the drive. It's a strange thing. Mindy and Zoey in the back enjoying each other's company. Samantha happily sitting there as Zoey sings and pets her. The road is easy, no traffic, and few cars block our way. A quiet Sunday drive, but I'm not sure it's Sunday right now. Regardless of that, I see myself settling into the lifestyle. A family, one I've never had before. I could come to enjoy this type of life.

Carl's truck pulls up beside us with Jill's window rolled down. She's making a motion for me to do the same. I comply.

"Back a bit one of the campers is having problems," Jill calls out, arm stretched and finger pointing back.

I look in a mirror. A camper is pulled over to the side a little way back. I nod to Jill and slow down. Carl slows as well and makes a U-turn. I start to follow as a horse with a rider come out of the brush on the south side of the road. The rider, long black hair streaming behind him, throws a lit bottle at our truck. It smashes on the hood and explodes in a ball of fire.

20

SHARE A RIDE

Fire erupts on the hood of the truck. Flames lick at the windshield. Mindy and Zoey scream. I swerve right, then left. Metal complains as it bends against another car. I slam on the breaks. Tires grab the road and we screech to a stop. I throw the vehicle into park and shove open the door.

"Out! Now!"

Samantha jumps out of the car and I pull open the rear door to get both of the girls to safety. Carl's truck skids to a stop a few metres away. Both of them are out of the vehicle. Jill levels her AR but the horse and rider are gone.

Others of our convoy stop. The big campers come to a lumbering halt. The truck smoulders from a small fire on the hood but nothing else has happened to it.

Both Mindy and Zoey are out of the vehicle and we scramble to Carl's truck.

Jill's head pivots as she scans the horizon, Glock in hand. "Who the hell was that?"

"Wish I could tell you." I take out my gun and check to make sure it's good to go. "He disappeared into the brush over there."

"I'm covering that area," Jill says.

Mindy leans against the truck. Her breath comes in short gasps. "Why would someone do that?"

The thought of someone doing such, especially with the state of the world, is confusing. Information just rolls through my mind and still, nothing screams at me.

"We're near Chippewa land here." Carl drops his arms, holsters his gun. "Notice the lack of corpses? Could be the tribe is making a move to claim the area back."

It doesn't make sense to me. They're a peaceful people. Nothing bad ever happened between the islanders and the rest of us in the area before.

"I don't understand why they would do something like this." I watch as the flames start to die as the lonely camper rolls up with a spare tire on the front. Must have been a flat.

The mid-day sun beats down on us as the temperature rises. There's nothing we can do about what happened, just move on and see if we can make it to the area we decided on.

Carl and I look the truck over to make sure there's no real damage, just cosmetic – and I don't care how it looks. Samantha is the other problem, but Zoey finds her cowering in the ditch. It takes a while to catch her, but she comes to Zoey after a few minutes. A rifle fires in the background.

"We got company," someone in the group calls out. "Lots of them coming out from the south side of the road."

Carl and I spin to look in the direction indicated. Between the trucks we see a group of corpses stumble out of the brush from the side of the road. More than we have time to drop before they're upon us.

"We have to move, now." I pull out the keys for the truck and head to it.

Mindy steps toward the vehicle and hesitates, hand reaching for the door. "Is the truck safe?"

"Yes," Carl says. "Only a surface burn on the hood. It was probably old gas or something."

Mindy nods but doesn't climb in. Instead, she holds back with Zoey while I start the vehicle.

The truck turns over right away and without any issues. I roll down the window and smile at the girls. "Looks like it's okay. Climb in."

We're just past Park Road. Still a lot of driving to do before we near the town of Beaverton. Virginia Beach is the next largest area to drive past, and it may hold corpses. We move out.

More cars litter the sides of the road. It's like people pulled over to let others pass and then couldn't get going again. All the corpses in the vehicles are dead, meaning not moving. Each has either a bullet hole taking out the brain or part of the head removed. The car doors aren't open. It's like a graveyard driving along forty-eight and we're not welcome to stop. A shiver starts at the base of my neck, radiating outward, down my legs and arms. Hair rises on my limbs. I keep scanning the road in front of us for any sign of problems.

Virginia Beach fades into the rear-view mirror and I finally breathe again. Mindy puts her hand on my shoulder. The soft reassurance of getting through that area is nice. We just have to get to Side road twenty-three and we're into Beaverton.

Everyone decided the direct route would be the best. Get into town, find the barge, then get to the island. My concern is the last part. That includes Mom and Doc, no matter how long it takes them to do what she wanted to.

The old drive-in theatre sits to the left of us as we snake our way through a crash site. Several vehicles are crunched up on each other with only one path through them. Even the side of the road is blocked. There's just enough room for us to squeeze past, which is a concern for me. I hate bottlenecks.

One of the campers peels off and takes the driveway to the theatre. It's clear of cars and someone inside the vehicle waves. A concussive explosions sounds. The front end lifts into the air. Fire erupts from underneath. It comes down as the wave from the explosion hits the truck.

I slam on the breaks, bring the truck to a stop, and jump out at a dead run toward the camper.

Carl must be out of his truck, his voice hitting me from behind. "Stop!"

I don't listen to him. The people in the camper need help. Fire strokes the side of the vehicle, threatening to engulf the whole thing. I'm tackled from behind, landing face first into the grass. My nose is centimetres from a half-buried jumble of tight wires. I reach out to pull the object from the ground but Carl clamps a big hand on my wrist.

"Don't. Looks like an IAD." He lets go of my hand. "Someone's mined the area."

Carl gets off and offers a hand. I take it.

"What the hell, Carl?"

He hunches down and stares at the device. "There may be more of them. Watch where you step."

There's a command in his voice I've not heard before. He takes two steps beyond the IAD and stops, bends, and steps over another one. There's a train of seven men and two women following us.

I'm counting the seconds as they turn into minutes. "This is taking too long."

The fire licks the sky, rolling up to the front of the camper. Fuel line may have ruptured. It may not light up like regular but it will still burn.

"We'll get there, just a few metres." Carl steps over another, then another. Soon we're onto the theatre drive. It's overrun by brush due to non-usage over the last seven years but still driveable.

We get to the vehicle. Carl pulls open the door and rushes in. I follow. He dashes to the front, I go to the back. This one's carrying some of the women from the biker's brothel.

Two women in the back are holding on to each other, shaking. Shock possibly. They've been through a lot and now this explosion. I motion them forward and hold out a hand. One starts to come forward but the other pulls her back.

"We don't have time for this," I mutter. "We need to get out of the camper and get you two safe."

Both have recognized me and the braver of the two tugs the other off the back bed. They come forward and hug me, making it hard to move. I loosen their grips and turn to see Carl pulling the woman from the passenger seat out the door.

"This way," I say, walking toward the door. "Don't run from the camper. There're mines out there and we need to get you safe."

It takes too long to get the women moving. Carl enters the camper and starts to work on getting the driver out of the seat.

"You're not injured, get to the door." I pull their arms from me.

Once free, I rush over to Carl and the driver.

The man's face is a mess of cuts from broken glass and a smashed nose. Probably the air bag caused some of the damage. The mass of pulp in the middle of his face has enraged his eyes. The two lids are swollen shut. The right side of his face droops, must be a fractured cheek bone.

Carl points down the road. "I see a number of mines spread out. Could be some behind us for all we know."

I nod, step to the door. "Everyone, back the way we came. We've lost this camper." Fire draws my gaze toward it. "Need to clear out before it blows."

Everyone takes the hint and steps back from the vehicle, making their way to the main road. The two women are collected as they exit the camper and are led across as well. Mindy helps escort them away from the section. She's too close for comfort to the mines.

"What's taking so long?" I yell back to Carl.

He grunts. "Can't get the seat belt undone."

"Cut it. Vehicle's lost anyway."

I walk back to him and hold out a knife. He takes it and starts to cut. The belt is strong, but the knife is sharp. It makes quick work of the binding. Carl has the man free fast. Together we lift him out of the chair and he ends up on my shoulders in a fireman's carry. Carl helps lead me out of the vehicle and across the mine field.

One of the front tires blows. Nitrogen fills the air with a stale taste. I hunch over at the sound. It's like a small bomb going off. One metre in front of the vehicle another mine erupts in a fireball. The camper's done.

I keep second-guessing myself as we drive up Lake Ridge Road. Could we have avoided the problems if we hadn't taken this road to begin with? It would have been simple, just drive east until we reached Highway twelve and go from there. But no, I had to come up with a different place, something that got a few of us dead. Now I'll have to live with that for the rest of my life. A leader needs to have a good plan to start with, and this one's gone to shit.

The road bends toward tenty-three and cars are blocking our path. Not much can be done at this point so I slow. We can turn around and go back to forty-eight, make our way through there. A route we just abandoned for this one. The plan is evolving back to what I originally had in mind.

Mindy taps me on the shoulder. "What's going on?"

"Cars blocking our way. Need to double everyone back." I crank the wheel and the truck swings, but the road is too narrow for a full turn. The campers are going to have a hell of a time unless they can loop onto Queen and then Thorah Park. Not the best of ideas, that's a residential area. But, it is the only thing we can do.

Carl pulls up beside us, window down. "What's up?"

I point out the blockage and explain the plan. He adds we should go ahead of the campers, make sure the coast is clear. His ideas always fill the small details for me. It's why we make a good team.

He pulls over to the turn-off and drives down the road. I start to lose sight of him when he makes the left turn.

Giving directions to people is one of the most trying things I've had to do since the shit hit the proverbial fan. Everyone wants to know why we're turning around. Some want to inspect the barrier while others just want to run through it, damage be damned. I get to hear what others think of the turning around. We could turn right at the road and get behind the blockage. I don't think that's a good idea. There could be another block there just waiting, and no where to turn the campers around. Only a few say we're doing the right thing with going back to forty-eight.

Mindy steps up and talks to a number of people while I try to count out the anger building inside me. With a finger, she points to the protruding mound of a stomach and starts to pout. I don't know what to do with a crying pregnant woman, I can only guess it clinches the deal this these guys.

As the last camper makes its way down the cut off we hop into the truck and follow. Mindy is finally beside me, guess forgiveness is soon to come from the crap I put her through. Hope so, this has been a long few hours. Zoey is passed out in the back. I'm hoping none of this will affect her in the future.

We're lucky, the road back to Lake Ridge is clear of most issues. The odd corpse is slammed by a camper, and it appears Carl has cleared a few out of the way as well. There's not much excitement, just the way I wanted it to be. The camper in front of us turns onto Concession fourteen, cutting off some of the highway. It's a single lane road but what could go wrong now? Looks like we're finally going to make it.

There's blockage on Thorah Road just a few metres beyond forty-eight. Looks like we did the right thing by turning around. This highway is the best way to get into Beaverton and to the island. Nothing seems to be bad now. Noon approaches, so I think we should call an end to the trek. In a few hours our biggest worry will be getting the barge running and all the campers over the water. Not much of a problem. Diesel fuel will work for a number of years yet, and the barge runs on that… hopefully. We'll find out soon enough, even being the last vehicle in the convoy.

I glance over to Mindy and smile. Her eyes go wide and I turn toward the road. No problem there. She grunts. Puffs breath in and out for a second. Something's wrong but I don't know what it is. She grabs my hand and squeezes. I swear bones brake and crunch together.

There are times when I'm totally oblivious to what's happening, and I think this is one of them. I don't see the obvious, but something nags me enough that I pull over and park the truck.

"What's wrong?"

Sweat beads on Mindy's forehead. "I think my water broke." She holds up a hand covered in red.

I glance down. Blood covers her thighs. Something's wrong. We need Doc, but he's not here. It's too early and I don't know what to do.

Zoey peeks her head over the centre consul and turns her half-closed eyes toward me. "What's happening?"

"Mindy's going to have the baby," I say, opening the door and grabbing my rifle from the back."

"Cool," she says, eyes finally open fully like she had the greatest night's sleep.

"Grab me a blanket, will you?" Mindy says to Zoey. Her voice strains. She's trying to keep calm, but I hear the edge that screams panic.

Around the truck, I open Mindy's door. The seat goes back to recline her. We need someone to delivery this child, and it looks like I'm the volunteer.

"You'll need to take my pants off," Mindy says. "Get me a pair of clean–Ugghhh!"

There's nothing that's trained me for this situation. Doc gave me books but I never read them. I send Zoey into the back to grab stuff from the bags and bring them up. She's going to be a nurse today, and that leaves me as the doctor. My hands shake. I don't know what to do.

The contractions are far apart, but all the shows I watched told me that can change at any time. I dare not move us for fear of the child arriving while we're driving. Frantic, I need to figure this out. It's a problem and I'm a problem solving person. Caution, that's the best way to look at it. And even with the large cabin of the truck there's not enough room for me to manoeuvre around Mindy's raised legs. I want to get her on the road but that's not a good response in the middle of nowhere.

Mindy grits her teeth. "God!"

The others should notice we're not behind them. I take her hand. Maybe they'll turn around and come back to help. Mindy crushes my fingers. There are some women in the group who've had children, they could do this instead of the IT guy. It's like she wants me to feel the same level of pain she's having.

Time flies. A little over an hour passes since the contractions started and they're closer together. Still no vehicles on their way. Why hasn't anyone noticed we're not behind them?

Mindy lets out a breath. "I don't know how much more of this I can take."

"We could go to that house." Zoey points up a dirt road. A small gate is across it with a No Trespassing sign. Great. The house looks like one of those small portable ones, but it's better than the truck.

Short intakes of breath fill the air as Mindy tries to imitate women from the TV shows.

"Hold on." I close the door. In a flash, I'm around and back in the driver's seat, starting the truck. Got to get her safe. Someplace we can be secure. The house is the only thing standing between shelter and no shelter.

"What're you doing?" Mindy calls out.

"Getting us safe." The gate crashes to the side as I drive through it heading for the house. Bet it's full of corpses, that's been my luck for the last little while. "Zoey, I'll need you to make sure Mindy's good while I clear out the house."

"Okay." A smile wider than her face appears.

Mindy lets out another scream. I swear her contractions are closer now. At least, I hope so. The closer together the better chance of less complications I would think.

We stop just in front of the place. The best sign I've seen all day is the closed door and intact windows. There's no car in the drive and that's another good indication the house is secure. I pull up and park, scan the horizon for anything coming toward us. Mindy grunts. She's bearing down. The baby's coming now and there's nothing I can do to stop it.

Zoey stands up in the back. "What should I do?"

I'm around the truck and there beside Mindy. There are several things I can think of but one sticks out, I put her feet on the dash and pull off her panties.

"Looks like here is the place it's going to happen." I try to smile at Mindy.

"Fuck! This hurts!" Mindy bears down again. Contractions are just seconds apart now. She's giving birth.

I look down, our child's head is crowning. There's blood. A thick mucus of white spots the pink skin underneath. Our child is coming out. I touch the head. Mindy grunts. She pushes. Her hair is plastered against her cheekbones. My child's head pops out and I grab it, gently supporting while Mindy pushes. One arm comes free, a line of blood traces down it. Another arm. One final push and Mindy frees the child from her body. The cord pulses and mucus spills from her mouth. A little cry escapes as I place our daughter on Mindy's chest. "We have a girl."

Looks like things are going to be all right after all.

ABOUT DOUGLAS OWEN

Douglas Owen is a writer, author, editor, and publisher. He is the owner of DAOwen Publications in Canada.

Doug spends most of his time working with authors and publishing, but he also writes a column in the online magazine InD'-tale called A Written View. He's also a member in good standing with the Writers' Community of York Region.

When Doug is not writing you can find him fishing with friends or cooking for his wife.

Doug lives in a rural hide-a-way in Goodwood, Ontario with his wife and their three cats.

Visit Doug's website at:
Life is but a Blog
(https://daowen.ca)

 facebook.com/AuthorDouglasOwen

 twitter.com/Douglas_A_Owen

instagram.com/daowenca

ALSO BY DOUGLAS OWEN

Broken World Series

Book I - The Hordes

Book II - The Family

Inside My Mind: Volume I

Inside My Mind: Volume II

The Spear Series

Book I - A Spear In Flight

Book II - A Sharp Spear Point

Book III - Slashed by a Spear Shaft